The
Dragonslayer's
Apprentice

DAVID CALDER

Interior illustrations by
Stieg Retlin

SCHOLASTIC INC.
New York Toronto London Auckland Sydney
Mexico City New Delhi Hong Kong

POINT FANTASY

*As this book has been reprinted word for word from the original
New Zealand edition, readers will find that standard British
spelling of words occurs throughout the text.*

If you purchased this book without a cover, you should be aware
that this book is stolen property. It was reported as "unsold and
destroyed" to the publisher, and neither the author nor the
publisher has received any payment for this "stripped book."

No part of this publication may be reproduced in whole or in part,
or stored in a retrieval system, or transmitted in any form or by any
means, electronic, mechanical, photocopying, recording, or otherwise, without written permission of the publisher. For information
regarding permission, write to Scholastic New Zealand Ltd.,
Private Bag 94407, Greenmount, Auckland 1730, New Zealand.

ISBN 0-590-63093-8

Text copyright © 1997 by David Calder.
Illustrations copyright © 1998 by Scholastic Inc.
All rights reserved.
Published by Scholastic Inc., 555 Broadway, New York, NY 10012,
by arrangement with Scholastic New Zealand Ltd.
SCHOLASTIC, POINT, and associated logos are trademarks
and/or registered trademarks of Scholastic Inc.

12 11 10 9 8 7 6 5 4 3 2 1   8 9/9 0 1 2 3/0

Printed in the U.S.A.   01

First Scholastic printing, December 1998

Editor: Penny Springthorpe

Cover illustration by Randy Hamblin

For my granddaughters and
step-grandchildren

Kylie and Talia (Wanganui)

Cliff and Matthew (Hamilton)

Rachael, James and Anna-Claire (Christchurch)

and

Sophie and Ngaire (Horsham, England)

I

The Dragonslayer stopped and looked down on the town at the river mouth. Behind him his assistant, Ron, and new apprentice, Jackie, also reined in and looked down.

The Dragonslayer wasn't seeing the town. He was thinking about his new apprentice. A girl. He had taken on a girl. Not even a woman. A girl. A teenage girl. He was mad, quite mad. She had been very persuasive, but even so he was stark-staring, raving mad.

"Is that where it is?" she asked now.

"What?" he said absent-mindedly.

"The 'rampaging beast'," she said.

"What? Oh, yes. Beast. Yes, that's where it's supposed to be. Can't see it though. Can you, Ron?"

Hearing no answer, the Dragonslayer turned in time to catch Ron shaking his head.

"I wish you would use words when I'm not looking at you," he said. I do pick them, he thought. An assistant who doesn't speak two words a day, and a girl. He nudged his horse into movement again. "Come on. Let's find the mayor and see what he wants done."

As they rode down the hill, a small boy came out of a line of trees on a pony and galloped away toward the town. The Dragonslayer wondered if he was a lookout.

He was. The mayor met them at the town boundary, accompanied by most of his council and half his staff. Apart from being tall and dark, he looked rather ordinary.

At least he doesn't look pompous, thought the Dragonslayer.

Looks can be deceptive.

"We welcome you in the name of the Borough of Westhaven," proclaimed the mayor. "We, the leading citizens of this, the fairest borough on the western coast, are gathered here to welcome you . . ."

"That's two 'welcome's in thirty-three words," the Dragonslayer heard Jackie whisper. "If he goes on like this, we'll be the most welcome people in history."

". . . and I am joined in this welcome . . ."

"Three," said Jackie, no longer whispering.

"Quiet, he'll hear you," snapped the Dragonslayer.

"So?" said Jackie, whispering again. "He doesn't know what I'm talking about. I whispered the first part."

"Just stop it," begged the Dragonslayer. "He's the man who's going to give us the job. Or not. And pay us. Or not."

". . . you come at a most opportune time and are truly most welcome," continued the mayor.

The Dragonslayer found himself straining to hear a voice saying 'four'. He wasn't sure if he heard it or not.

"The very future and prosperity of our town is threatened. The lives of its citizens are threatened. The municipal facilities that have made our name a byword on this coast are threatened. Our prosperity is being destroyed. The tourist trade is dwindling. People could be killed. Our prosperity is threatened."

"That's three threats to prosperity to two threats to people," said Jackie.

"Will you be *quiet*!" hissed the Dragonslayer.

The mayor appeared to be almost finished. "So, if you can dispose of this great threat to our prosperity, our amenities, our tourist trade, our prosperity, our livelihoods," he said, "we will be eternally grateful."

"And more prosperous," added Jackie.

"We thank you for your welcome," said the Dragonslayer. "We have had a long and tiring journey, but we're used to that. You have need of our services and we hastened to do your bidding. You make us most welcome. We . . ." he had a sudden impression of the young girl counting his 'welcome's and his voice died. Her giggle didn't help. "We don't see any sign of the rampaging beast . . ." he added, and again faded out as he realised that he had used her phrase.

"The beast has wandered off into the countryside," the mayor said, "but it'll be back. It always comes back. It likes knocking down brightly coloured buildings. Or very tall ones. Or ones that just happen to be in its way. It's destroying our prosperity, our amenities, our buildings . . ."

"No people at all this time," said Jackie.

"*Quiet!*" yelled the Dragonslayer.

"I was only trying to explain . . ." began the mayor in a hurt voice.

"Not you. My apprentice. New. Not trained properly." He turned to Jackie. "If you cost us this job," he snapped, "I'll cancel your apprenticeship."

The threat silenced her. The Dragonslayer realised that Jackie didn't know that the only way he could void her contract was by applying to the Dragonslayers' Guild and the Apprentices' Guild, and facing hearings before the Apprentice Contracts Appeal Board and the Apprentice Contracts Appeal Board Appeal Authority, none of which he had time for anyway.

"Could we go to our quarters?" the Dragonslayer asked the mayor. "We need to meet your experts and then there'll be quite a bit of planning to do. Tactics. Strategies. You know."

He was deliberately vague. In jobs like this, you had to play it by ear. If you announced a plan in advance, then changed it, you were just buying an argument. And if the modified plan didn't work, they would argue about payment, even if you did eventually kill their dragon, or giant, or strange beast. Or drive out their witch. Or whatever.

"Certainly," said the mayor. "Nothing is too good for the gallant men, er, gallant band that is going to drive away this threat to our fair town."

"And restore your prosperity," said Jackie.

"Indeed," he said, beaming at her. "Very perceptive young woman you have there," he said to the Dragonslayer. "Your daughter?"

"Apprentice," said the Dragonslayer.

"Oh," said the mayor. "That's unusual. We don't see many female apprentice dragonslayers in these parts."

"You don't see *any*," said Jackie sweetly. "If you had any dragonslayers of your own, with or without female apprentices, you wouldn't be calling on us."

The mayor looked at her coldly. "No," he said, and turned back to the Dragonslayer. "Are you sure you can deal with the beast?"

"Of course," said the Dragonslayer.

Confidence. First rule of negotiating, as his late father had always said. Mind you, confidence had killed him in the end. Or over-confidence. It really was his own fault, taking on two dragons single-handedly. A male and a female. In the mating season.

Later the Dragonslayer met with the town council staff

10

while Ron unpacked and checked their equipment. Jackie was sent out to inspect damage, more to get her out of the way during the talks than in the hope that she would discover anything of value.

When the senior staff assembled, the Dragonslayer was surprised to see how many there were. The mayor introduced the director of technical services, the director of planning, the director of surface communications (which turned out to be roading), the director of civic amenities, and eight other directors. The Dragonslayer lost track of who was what.

He hoped that, behind their elaborate titles, they knew their jobs. It took him a long time to find out.

Every time he asked for information a director gave it to him, then explained that anything he said was subject to the views of any colleagues whose areas of responsibility impinged on his own. Then several other directors would each take five minutes to explain that their responsibilities did indeed impinge, but that they endorsed everything their colleague had said. Then all the other directors would explain that their responsibilities did not impinge, but they supported their colleague anyway.

The Dragonslayer noticed that it took each of the latter about ten mintues to say, in effect, that they had nothing to say. Why don't they have a meeting with the beast and just *bore* it to death, he thought.

It finally emerged that repeated attempts had been made to drive the beast away. That was no problem — fire, noise and numbers of people all worked — but it always came back.

"What does it eat?" the Dragonslayer asked.

Anything, he was told.

"Killed anybody?"

No, they admitted, it hadn't actually killed anybody. They sounded almost disappointed, as if it had no business to be doing so much damage without loss of life.

"What do you actually want me to do?" he asked.

Kill it, of course, they said.

The directors made it obvious that if he didn't know that was what he was expected to do, he couldn't be much of a dragonslayer.

"I have to be sure," he explained. "Sometimes people want them captured alive; sometimes they just want them driven off. Sometimes they want the problem transferred to a rival town. I don't do that. Against guild ethics. But you'd be surprised how often it comes up."

"*No!*" chorused the officials. They looked shocked, in a practiced kind of way.

"Do you want the skin?" he asked.

No, they didn't want the skin. They looked puzzled.

"That's something else we often get asked for," he explained. "The skin to be preserved. Some councils want it to make mayoral robes, or to upholster council chamber seating or some such. Costs more if I have to kill it without damaging the pelt."

Just kill it, they told him.

"Right. Have any attempts been made already?"

No, it appeared not. They had too much sense to get in close. They didn't think they were scared. Just prudent.

"After all," said one director, "we're not professionals in that area. That's why we've commissioned you."

"Indeed, it's no work for amateurs," said the Dragonslayer, and kept to himself his profound relief that he wouldn't be dealing with a beast already injured and in pain, and savage and unpredictable as a result.

Ron came in, caught his eye and nodded. The

Dragonslayer translated Ron's nod in his mind: "I've unpacked the equipment, checked it, sharpened everything, made repairs where necessary, oiled everything, laid it out in order and locked it up safely."

"Thank you," the Dragonslayer said, and meant it. A good man, Ron. Short on words, but a good man.

The conference ended with an agreement that the Dragonslayer and his crew would go out the following morning with the director of technical services to find the beast and make a preliminary assessment of the problem.

At first all twelve directors insisted that it was absolutely essential that they go too. So many areas of responsibility are involved, they said. The Dragonslayer pointed out that having so many could lead to loss of life, and eleven of them immediately agreed enthusiastically that it was only the director of technical services whose presence was absolutely essential. The director of technical services also agreed, but without any enthusiasm at all.

II

The Dragonslayer asked Ron if their quarters were close and suitable, if food was available, and if there were any problems. Ron confirmed that everything was satisfactory. That is, he nodded. And Jackie arrived back.

"Well," said the Dragonslayer, "did you discover anything useful?"

She began talking and it was several seconds before what she was saying sank in. He suddenly realised that he should pay attention.

". . . the damaged buildings are mostly single-storey wooden houses. There's little or no significant damage to stone buildings, even though it's obviously had a go at them. Bigger wooden buildings have been attacked, but usually only in one place, not completely demolished. The beast is almost . . ."

"What?" said the Dragonslayer.

"Casual," said Jackie.

"Casual?" the Dragonslayer snapped. "You heard the mayor. It's done severe damage to this town and you say it's casual? What on earth do you mean?"

It was Jackie's turn to snap. "If you give me half a chance, I'll tell you." She paused to make him invite her to continue, and with rather bad grace he did so.

"Have you ever walked along with a stick in your hand, just slashing at clumps of grass and bushes?" she asked. "That's exactly what the pattern of damage looks like. Buildings haven't been flattened deliberately. At least it doesn't look like it. It looks more like a walk down a street with a few casual swipes left and right."

The following morning, when he saw the damage for himself, the Dragonslayer realised what a perceptive report it had been. Jackie caught him looking at her thoughtfully.

They didn't have to go far to see the beast; it was on its way back into town. They could hear the crashing and yelling quite plainly. They went straight down the road for two blocks and there it was.

"Why, it's just a kitten," said Jackie.

"It's twice the size of an elephant," said the director of technical services.

"But I was right," she said. "It's only being playful, not deliberately destructive."

"It just knocked down another house!"

"But it didn't really mean to."

"The house is just as flat as if it did mean to."

"This debate is fascinating," said the Dragonslayer, "but it isn't killing the beast."

"Do we have to?" asked Jackie.

"Yes," said the Dragonslayer and the director together.

"*Can* you kill it?" the director asked the Dragonslayer.

"Yes." He knew they could, though he was not yet sure exactly how.

"Then kill it right now," said the director.

"You don't want that," said the Dragonslayer.

"Don't I? Why not?"

"Do you want to move it once it's dead? Or perhaps you just want to leave it there."

"No. But don't you . . ."

"No," said the Dragonslayer. "Standard contract. Disposal of remains to be the responsibility of the party of the first part. That's you. Party of the second part — that's me — to be responsible for rendering subject —

17

that's the beast, in this case — into the condition required by the party of the first part. That means dead. After that, you take over."

"Oh," said the director. "What do you suggest then?"

"We entice it to the place where we want it killed. Or as near as we can get."

"How do we — er, you — do that?"

"Food usually works, but it doesn't seem hungry."

"It's not," said a man in the crowd who had been listening to them. "It eats grass and other plants, browses off trees, knocks over rubbish bins and eats what it can find. It's always eating, but I doubt it's hungry enough for food to be much of an enticement."

"There's always something," said the Dragonslayer, though he couldn't at the moment think what it might be. The other possibilities were a mate, or a captured youngster, but this one didn't seem to have either. Then he remembered that it was easily driven.

"Where do you want it killed?" he said.

The director of technical services didn't even have to think. "At the rubbish dump," he said, "if you can get it there, and especially if you position it properly. All we'll have to do then is cover it up."

"I want a dozen men with flaming torches," said the Dragonslayer. "Good, reliable types who'll obey orders and not panic if the beast does something unexpected." Like tramples some of them, he thought.

The director didn't think that was too much trouble. "We should be able to assemble that many from staff. Of course, I'll come myself."

The Dragonslayer thanked him. The director looked as if he would much rather have had his offer rejected.

They had forgotten Jackie. "Do we have to kill it?" she asked again.

"Yes," said the Dragonslayer.

The director didn't join in this time. He was too busy thinking about getting close to the beast, flaming torch or no flaming torch.

"If I can find a way to rid the town of the beast without us having to kill it, will you try?" Jackie asked the Dragonslayer.

"Provided I still get paid for whatever we do, yes," he said. "What did you have in mind?"

"Don't know yet," she said.

The Dragonslayer turned to Ron and asked him if he had any ideas. Ron said he couldn't think of any way of disposing of the beast without killing it, that any attempt to do so would be extremely dangerous, and he didn't think Jackie would think of anything. That is, he shook his head.

"How soon do you want the men," asked the director. "Us, that is."

"This afternoon, if possible," said the Dragonslayer. "No point in waiting. It'll only do more damage."

"Yes, of course. This afternoon. Why not? I'll assemble the men."

The Dragonslayer left to sign a formal contract with the mayor and council, the director went to assemble his men, and Jackie went off on some private business of her own. Ron stood watching the beast and the crowd, nodding to no one in particular every so often.

The director returned two hours later with eleven men and twelve torches, soon to be flaming.

Jackie came back and waited for the Dragonslayer to notice her. When he didn't, she spoke up. "Remember what you said?"

"What? No, I don't. What was it?"

"That if I found a way of getting rid of the beast without killing it, you'd consider it."

The Dragonslayer thought rapidly. He had signed a standard contract, to 'kill or *dispose* of the aforesaid beast to the satisfaction of the party of the first part'. So he didn't *have* to kill it.

"You remember the circus that was at the town where we met?" Jackie continued. "Well, I've been in touch and they'll be happy to have the beast. They say they know what it is, and it's young enough to be trained and" — she lowered her voice and glanced at the director who was standing a short distance off — "they say they'll pay for it, cash on delivery."

"No," said the Dragonslayer.

"Oh please, please."

"No."

"Why not?"

He ticked off the points on his fingers. "Firstly, there's the problem of transport. What do you propose to do, build a cage? Put a halter on it and lead it? And if you built a cage, how would you transport that? And we cannot accept payment for it, other than genuine expenses, if we've already accepted payment from the town. Guild rules."

"The circus said they'll come and get it," said Jackie.

"Will they now," said the Dragonslayer.

Doing something other than simply killing the beast was starting to look like a professional challenge to the Dragonslayer. It really was worth considering. Most dragonslayers killed. If you knew what you were doing, it was both the simplest and the safest option. But most dragonslayers remained anonymous tradesmen all their lives. It was the ones with a bit of panache who were invited to deliver papers at dragonslayer conventions and who were mentioned in the honours list. Capturing this beast and handing it over to a circus definitely had possibilities.

"What do we have to do?" he asked Jackie. "We can't just tell them to come and get it. The town wouldn't pay us, and we couldn't ask —"

"Guild rules?" asked Jackie.

"Of course," he said, and wondered why she grinned.

"There isn't really a problem," she said.

"Isn't there?" He was sure he could do it, but hardly without problems. It might in fact be the challenge of his professional career. He would have to keep careful notes of his methods and techniques. It would be the first time he had attempted to capture anything this size.

A few baby dragons hardly counted. The largest had scarcely been the size of a big crocodile and it was barely able to generate the black vapour that everyone always thought was smoke. It wasn't, and there was certainly never any fire, though everyone always imagined there was. The more imaginative survivors of close encounters even claimed to have been singed.

He dragged his thoughts back to the present. The first task was to drive the beast out of town and along to the rubbish dump. That would give him time to think what to do next. He had a sudden idea.

"Has it ever found its own way to the rubbish dump?" he asked the director.

"No. It wanders out into the countryside sometimes, but it never leaves town on that side. We're not sure why, but it might be discouraged by the belt of trees in that direction. It's more open everywhere else."

"Plenty to eat at the dump?"

The director shrugged. "You know rubbish dumps."

"Here we go, then." The Dragonslayer called the men with the torches over. He explained what they had to do to get the beast moving, what to do if it turned on them, how to stop it going down side roads, what to do when they reached the dump. He warned against heroics: "One death is bad, but two or more is worse. If somebody gets hurt or killed, leave it to me. I'm the expert, remember." He said this more for reassurance than anything else. If there was a disaster, there wasn't much he or anybody else could do about it.

"Right. Light your torches and we'll get going," he said. "My assistant, that's Ron here, will be on the right of the line. I'll be in the middle and my apprentice, Jackie, will be with me. Forward!"

III

The beast was quite easy to drive, as the council staff had said. It didn't like fire and moved away from the torches whenever one came close. It gave an occasional swipe at a torch bearer, and the Dragonslayer found himself agreeing with Jackie that they were playful swipes, though they would have crushed anyone they hit.

The council staff were disciplined and efficient and they arrived at the town dump almost before the Dragonslayer realised it.

He called the men back and watched the beast for a few minutes. It was trotting around, obviously excited, probably by the smell of food. It soon began to root around in the rubbish and then to feed.

"I don't think I will kill it," said the Dragonslayer.

The director looked as if he was going to have a stroke. "But your contract!"

"To *dispose* of, not necessarily kill, is what the contract says. I know of a circus that's prepared to take it and I think I'll capture it and hand it over to them. It's a fine specimen, young enough to train. Not many of them round now. Endangered species. My colleagues are too efficient," he finished apologetically.

"What kind of beast is it, then?" asked the director. "We had the idea that nobody knew what it was."

"*Felis giganticus*," said the Dragonslayer hurriedly, "if I remember my zoology correctly. Been a long time, you know, and they really are rare these days." Must be, if I've never seen one before, he added to himself.

"But what are you going to do in the meantime?" the director said. "We don't want it wandering back into town. We don't even want it wandering around here. We do have to use the dump, you know."

"There's no problem," said the Dragonslayer. "We'll watch it here, make sure it doesn't wander off, and keep it away from your people when they come to dump rubbish. Might be an idea to close the dump to the public though, just to be safe."

"Have you noticed that it has beautiful eyes?" said Jackie to no one in particular.

"I've noticed that it knocks down buildings," said the director.

"Yes, but its eyes are beautiful. Big and brown and so deep you could sink right into them."

"If it would just sink into its own eyes, it would save us many problems," said the director.

The beast — Felix, as the Dragonslayer was beginning to think of it, derived from its hastily invented Latin name — was happily trotting around, nosing at things and eating, or trying to eat, almost everything it found. The beast really was young, he reflected, and playful. He quickly put an end to that sort of thinking. Get fond of it and it'll be hard to kill, if that's what we finally have to do, he thought.

Jackie and the director were arguing again.

"It would make a great town mascot and tourist attraction," said Jackie. "Just think what it could do for your prosperity."

"I prefer to have the houses," said the director. "What's the use of a tourist attraction without a town to accommodate the tourists? What's the use of prosperity without a town to be prosperous in?"

"Are you always so negative?"

"I don't call it being negative."

"What do you call it then?"

"Realistic."

Time for me to be realistic too, thought the Dragonslayer. They had got the beast out of the town and they had a reasonable prospect of keeping it there, but he wondered how they could manage to hand it over to the circus.

He called Ron over and explained the situation. "We've got to keep the beast under control for a few days. Have you given the matter any thought?"

Ron nodded. That meant he had been thinking about it, had some ideas for controlling the beast, and didn't see handing it over to the circus as being unduly difficult.

The Dragonslayer suggested to him that he decide which idea should be tried first, explain it in detail and start assembling whatever was needed to carry it out.

Ron nodded again.

When the Dragonslayer explained to the director of technical services what was happening, he immediately wanted to take over.

"The beast can't get through the belt of trees on the dump's boundary," the director said. "It should be simple enough to build a three-sided pen against the trees, lure the beast in and close the opening behind it."

"And what do you propose building the pen with?" the Dragonslayer asked.

"There's plenty of solid rubbish around — old wagons in particular — and the council's got plenty of strong fencing if it's required."

"Strong enough for that?" asked the Dragonslayer, nodding towards the beast.

"Yes," the director said.

I don't think so, the Dragonslayer thought, but he said nothing. It was usually quicker to let them try and fail than argue with them. And after a failure, they usually argued a great deal less.

A high, strong, three-sided pen was quickly built against the trees. The Dragonslayer was doubtful that it would hold the beast if it really put its mind to getting out, but there was no harm in trying.

Getting the beast into the pen was surprisingly easy. As soon as the men moved away, its curiosity took it inside the enclosure and they quickly closed the opening behind it.

"There, what could be simpler than that?" said the director.

"It'll climb out," said Jackie.

"It can't," said the director.

The beast climbed out.

Jackie grinned. Some of the men laughed.

The director went very red in the face. "Well," he said in a huff, "you better have a go yourselves. See if you can do any better."

The Dragonslayer had some ideas of his own. He also had a high regard for Ron's ingenuity, but he wished Ron had been a bit more explicit. Nods and shakes of the head were all right as far as they went, but at moments like these they didn't go far enough.

Ron had disappeared, but the Dragonslayer was able to tell the townspeople that he had been sent on an important errand. Provided Ron didn't take too long, all would be well. And with luck he would come back with a good idea, and even the equipment to carry it out.

Ron came back looking very pleased with himself. The Dragonslayer showed him the pen and told him it had been unsuccessful. "Do you have a better idea?" he asked Ron. "And if so, could we start on it at once?"

"Yes," said Ron, then wandered away on what looked like a casual stroll around the dump.

Why, the Dragonslayer wondered to himself, did Ron convey so much less when he finally did speak than when he just nodded or shook his head?

Ron proceeded to explain, without words, that the pen had been too small. Confine the beast to the whole dump and there would be no problem. There would be plenty of room, plenty of food, plenty to amuse it. What more could it want?

What indeed?

"But," the Dragonslayer said, "how are we going to confine it to the dump? Practically one whole side's open."

Ron grinned and pointed to the torches used to drive the beast, now put out and neatly piled. Then he pointed to an imaginary series of evenly spaced points across the open side.

The Dragonslayer grasped the idea immediately: a

row of burning torches set in the ground; a man, two at the most, to tend them and keep an eye on things. Yes, it would work. Two men could easily confine the beast with torches while council staff dumped loads of rubbish.

The Dragonslayer went back to the director. "We've solved all the problems," he said, and explained what they were going to do.

The director raised a few routine objections, as a man whose own idea hasn't worked naturally does, and finally agreed that there didn't seem to be any obvious fault in the plan. They set up the torches, and the director organised two men to look after them and keep an eye on the beast. The circus men wouldn't arrive until the following morning.

After their evening meal, the Dragonslayer, Jackie and Ron went for a walk around the town. They found, as usual when things were going well, that they were celebrities. Everybody smiled and nodded and spoke. Ron nodded back and the Dragonslayer smiled and wished everybody well. Jackie loved it and soon found herself the centre of a group of young people. The Dragonslayer and Ron didn't see her again until they got back to their quarters.

*

The next morning they were woken far earlier than they expected. The circus men had arrived and wanted to get the beast loaded so they could start back immediately. The Dragonslayer complained, Jackie grumbled and Ron said nothing but managed to convey far more disapproval than anybody else.

The men had brought a big, stout, wheeled cage that could have held something far more formidable than the beast, which it apparently had if the teeth marks were anything to go by.

The Dragonslayer routed out the director ("Why should he sleep if we can't?") who took about an hour to assemble his team, while the circus men stood around and told tall-sounding stories about fearsome beasts and gave the impression that nothing was too much for a good keen circus team. They looked at the beast, said there was no problem, gave a few crisp orders and ten minutes later had the beast in the cage.

The beast got a bit upset when it realised it couldn't get out, but settled down quite well when they gave it some food. The circus manager was delighted, paid reasonable expenses and they all parted on excellent terms.

"Good people to do business with," the Dragonslayer said to Ron and Jackie. "We must remember them in future. Could be quite a useful sideline, providing beasts for circuses. Not always possible, of course. Where a beast has killed people there's usually a very strong desire to see it dead, but where capture is a possibility, we should bear it in mind. Good business. Good economics."

"Builds prosperity," said Jackie.

The Dragonslayer gave her a suspicious look, but her smile was perfectly innocent. Or seemed to be.

They went back to the council chambers and accepted payment. At first the mayor argued about the beast not being killed as provided for in the contract, but the town manager pointed out the 'kill or dispose of' clause in the contract.

"The Dragonslayer and his gallant team," the manager said, bowing toward Jackie, "have done everything they contracted to do."

With his most professional smile, the mayor expressed his deep gratitude, the council's deep gratitude, the gratitude of the staff and the approval of the citizens for all the Dragonslayer and his team had done to protect the town and preserve its buildings and amenities and its cultural heritage . . .

"And restore your prosperity," said Jackie.

The mayor handed over the cheque (and looked annoyed again when he realised that the town manager had made it out well in advance) and invited everybody to join him in a few drinks.

It turned out to be quite a party. The Dragonslayer, who liked to relax when a job had been well done, found that he and the mayor had quite a lot in common after all: they both liked whisky. After the first hour he had a confused impression of noise and colour and movement and endless talking, some of it in his own voice, and woke up in the morning with a nasty headache.

Jackie was disgustingly cheerful. "Wonderful party," she enthused. "Plenty of food, great people, lots of interesting conversation. And Ron made a speech."

"Ron - made - a - speech?" The Dragonslayer spoke in the same careful way that he would use to announce the end of the world. "You better tell me about it."

"Well, there was all this food, really nice . . . do you remember?"

"Yes," said the Dragonslayer, who didn't.

"But Ron only seemed interested in the sausage rolls and —"

"Yes, hard man on sausage rolls, is our Ron. But he doesn't usually make speeches about them."

"He did this time. Anyway, he ate a whole plate of them and —"

"That's nothing for Ron," said the Dragonslayer.

"Do you want to hear the speech or not?" said Jackie crossly. "You keep interrupting."

"Yes, tell me about the speech." The Dragonslayer was rapidly deciding that silence, as a way of life, had much to recommend it.

"Well," continued Jackie, "he'd just finished the last sausage roll when a young woman came up with another plateful. She was good-looking, in a blonde sort of way. Ron looked as if he thought so anyway. She held out the plate and said, 'Would you like another one?' And" — she paused dramatically — "and Ron said, 'Yes, I like them'."

"He can get very talkative when he's had a few drinks," said the Dragonslayer.

IV

The following morning the Dragonslayer reflected through his hangover that the operation had not been all that spectacular. He hardly needed the notes on method and technique, which in any case he had forgotten to make. There would be no prospects of scholarly papers at conventions, no mentions in the honours list from this exercise. Oh well, at least it was a start at doing something different. He'd be more switched on in future.

The letter offering another contract was brought in while he was still feeling unwell. It helped to know that there was another job to go to. Having to think about it didn't help at all, but the deputation was waiting and he had to make a decision.

He tried to read the letter, then he and Jackie went to meet the deputation. "What exactly is the threat?" he asked. "I mean, can you give me more detail than was in the letter from your illustrious" — he tried to remember how the letter had been signed but couldn't — "leader?" He thought that was a cunning way of covering up his inability to read the letter.

The leader of the deputation, a shrewd-looking older man who was deputy mayor of a village in the mountains, said, "It's a dragon. First one round our parts for generations. In fact, we thought they were extinct. Obviously not. It's killing our livestock and people."

"People last again," whispered Jackie.

The Dragonslayer winced.

"Did you say something?" inquired the deputy mayor, looking at Jackie coldly.

"I was just wondering what the name of your village was," said Jackie, who had seen it on the letterhead and wanted to hear him say it.

"High Nurking," he said.

With an effort, Jackie managed not to laugh. "Is it a

big dragon?" she asked, sensing that the Dragonslayer was losing touch.

"Big enough," said the deputy mayor.

"How big's that?" snapped Jackie. "They're big enough to be dangerous at one and a half metres, and they can grow to twelve metres. Some kinds, anyway. How big is this one?"

"It's killing stock and people and destroying buildings."

"Well, I'm glad people rank ahead of buildings," Jackie said, "even if they're behind stock. But please give us *some* idea of its length."

"Five metres."

The Dragonslayer dragged himself back into the conversation. "Has anyone tried to kill it?"

"Yes," said the deputy mayor. "One man. He was killed."

Amateurs, thought the Dragonslayer. What is it about dragons? People have enough sense to leave a giant beast or a huge bird alone, but if it's a dragon, they have to have a go. He knew why. It was the challenge, the same challenge that had made him become a dragonslayer, and his father before him.

"Has it settled down anywhere?" he asked.

"Seems so," said another man in the party, who was dressed in the plain clothes of a hunter. "It disappears up the mountain at the back of the village for two or three days at a time. We think it lives there."

"Sounds likely," said the Dragonslayer. It's probably found a cave, he thought. "And how many people has it killed?"

Only two, apparently. The first was a woman surprised at a mountain stream, and the second was the young man who had tried to kill it. Some others had had narrow escapes and bad frights. One man was injured in a fall as he ran away.

"What was it eating?" asked the Dragonslayer.

Cattle and sheep, mostly, they replied. The farmers had driven most of their stock into safe places, but not all were dragon-proof and the dragon was becoming increasingly bold. Because the farmers were superstitious and wouldn't stand guard at night, the dragon had learned to do most of its killing then.

It was obvious that the deputy mayor had no sympathy for superstition, and that the hunter and some others had a great deal. The atmosphere became a little tense. The

Dragonslayer tried to ease the tension by asking if the dragon was male or female.

The deputy mayor looked surprised, then puzzled, then said he didn't know. It was just a dragon.

"Male, you ignorant twit," said a voice at the back of the deputation. The deputy mayor flushed.

He's not very observant, thought the Dragonslayer, looking at the deputy mayor and trying to keep his face in focus. Probably didn't know what colour it was, either. But no harm in trying.

"What colour is it?" he asked.

"Greeny-blue," said the deputy mayor promptly.

Good, thought the Dragonslayer. Greeny-blue dragons were usually fairly docile (as dragons went). The black ones had nasty temperaments, for all their smaller size, and they were fiendishly clever.

"How long does it stay away, usually, when it goes up the mountain?" he asked.

"Two to three days on average," the deputy mayor said.

Good again, he thought. Didn't sound as if it had a mate on eggs. Would be hunting more often if it did.

The deputy mayor became impatient. "Will you come

quickly." It was a command, not a request. "We want it killed at once. It's doing us terrible harm. Now that the animals are hard to get at, it's much more aggressive. We don't want it rampaging through the village. We can't protect wooden houses against the fire."

There it is again, mused the Dragonslayer. Like everyone else, they think dragons breathe smoke, and where there's smoke there has to be fire . . .

"Yes, we'll come," he told the deputation. "First thing in the morning."

The deputy mayor started to protest, but the Dragonslayer cut him off. "We need time to check our gear and pack it, tie up a few loose ends here." And give my head time to recover, he thought.

The deputy mayor wasn't happy, but accepted it. "Do you have a staff?" he asked, looking as though he expected the answer to be no. He gave the council people a look that said 'lowland wimps' as plainly as if he had spoken it aloud.

"An assistant and an apprentice," said the Dragonslayer, indicating Jackie, and Ron, who had just joined them.

"A girl," said the deputy mayor.

"An apprentice," said the Dragonslayer.

"Oh well, I suppose you know your business."

"So does my apprentice," snapped the Dragonslayer, getting annoyed. His headache thumped.

The mayor of Westhaven knew a tense moment when he saw one. "Can we offer you hospitality?" he asked the men from High Nurking.

The diversion worked perfectly. The deputy mayor of High Nurking and his party accepted gratefully and the mayor led them off.

"You're getting a good man there," he told them.

"What about the girl?" asked the deputy mayor.

"Knows her job," said the mayor. "They all do. Especially the assistant. Doesn't say much, but he gets the job done." He paused, trying to remember if he had actually heard Ron speak. "Come to think of it, I don't think he actually says anything, but he's not what you'd call dumb."

Ron turned to the Dragonslayer and nodded, meaning that he and Jackie would check the equipment, repair it, sharpen it, stow it away and pack their personal gear ready to start early the next day. The Dragonslayer could go back to bed. The Dragonslayer accepted gratefully.

*

Next morning they started bright and early. The Dragonslayer, riding with the deputy mayor of High Nurking, found the morning quite bracing. The deputy mayor just found it cold. So, apparently, did everyone else. The next several mornings, as they climbed higher into the mountains, were colder still.

High Nurking was a picturesque village and the scenery was spectacular. There were no people in sight and they soon found out why: they had just missed the dragon. It had carried off several more cattle while the deputation had been seeking the Dragonslayer. It had become increasingly bold, and this time it had come right into the village.

Nobody had stayed around to argue. They had all taken refuge in their houses and didn't come out until they saw the deputy mayor and the strangers they hoped were the Dragonslayer and his party.

"Go and kill it!" screamed one woman. "It came right past my house. I thought my last day had come. Kill it! Kill it right now, before it comes back."

Even Jackie was quiet in the face of the fear that gripped the village. Killing dragons had promised to be fun. She hadn't expected it to be so deadly serious.

The Dragonslayer called the people around him and explained that the only thing worse than not trying to kill a marauding dragon was trying to kill it and failing. He explained that it made them cunning and very wary. That was when the hunter found himself being hunted — a very awkward situation, especially if the first he knew about it was dragon claws in his back.

He asked Ron to scout around and see if he could find which way the dragon had gone. Several people told him that it had gone up the mountain as usual, but they hadn't actually seen it.

Ron returned an hour later to report that the dragon had killed a deer at the foot of the mountain and had carried off the carcass. If it behaved as usual, it wouldn't be back for at least two days, plenty of time for the Dragonslayer to make his preparations.

It was three full days before anything happened. Because the villagers (Jackie referred to them as "Nurks") were friendly but not overly sociable, there was plenty of time in the evenings to sit and talk. As the Dragonslayer found out more about Jackie, he wondered whether he would have taken her on if he had known.

She was the daughter of a noble family and had been bored silly. "All I did was sit around all day, making polite conversation with courtiers and ladies-in-waiting," she said, and proceeded to mimic the conversations.

"Don't you think Lady Matilda's new gown is absolutely divine?"

I think it looks like a horse blanket.

"And doesn't it suit her?"

As a horse blanket, it does indeed.

"And the colour? Such an exquisite red."

It matches her complexion.

"And the weather, so changeable. Do you think it will rain?"

"If it doesn't stay fine, it may indeed rain. If it doesn't blow a gale. It could do both, of course. Oh dear, one never knows, does one?"

No, one never does, does one? Especially if one is an ignorant, small-minded twit whose world revolves around clothes and gossip.

"Have you heard? Lady Pamela is to marry Lord William? Who would have thought it? Isn't it exciting?"

It's only been obvious to everyone in the palace for the past six months. This is, if you happened to notice that they've spoken only to each other, have looked only at each other, and that the absence of one made the other quite impossible. That, and the poetry they've been writing to each other. And reciting aloud. Yes, I suppose if you missed all that, the fact that they're going to marry is something of a surprise.

"And have you seen Lord Robert's son, Sir Dudley Flapnoodle, back from university? So handsome! So polished!"

"Yes, indeed. And so very — how shall I put it? — hard to avoid."

So self-opinionated. So full of half-baked, second-hand ideas that he doesn't understand. So sure he is God's great gift to the state, the nobility, women, the human race. He's a complete idiot!

"And have you seen Lady Janet's twins lately? Such lovely, lively children."

"Yes indeed. They're so stimulating to have around. I'm sure they will go far."

And I hope the brats will go soon!

And so she had simply walked out. Actually, ridden out. Gone for a ride one day, slipped away from her ladies-in-waiting and kept going. She had taken some jewellery and sold it. That had given her enough money to live on for a while, and after trying a variety of jobs she had persuaded the Dragonslayer to take her on as an apprentice.

The Dragonslayer believed her story. Most of it, anyway. He wasn't too sure about the "noble family" bit. That was understating it, he thought. More like a royal one. He thought he remembered something about a missing princess a year or two back. One of the southern kingdoms? There could be problems.

"How old are you?" he asked her. "Your *real* age, if it's not the one you gave me. You're contracted now, and that gives you a fair amount of protection, but if you're younger than you said I need to know. If you're a *lot* younger, there may not be too much I can do. There are laws, you know."

"I'm sixteen," she told him, "like I said I was. That's not too young, is it?"

"No," said the Dragonslayer. "It makes you an adult for most purposes under the Agreed Laws of the United Kingdoms' Common Market. Might get tricky in your home kingdom, though. I mean, if your father happens to be on particularly good terms with the king, he might get a special dispensation if he really wants you back. Is he? On good terms with his king, I mean."

"Yes he is," said Jackie, "and I'm sure he wants me back. So yes, there could be a problem."

"Well, I won't ask you which kingdom," said the Dragonslayer, "but I want you to tell me if we cross the border. We don't want to upset him. The king, I mean. Or your father. Either of them. Do we?"

"No," agreed Jackie.

They looked at each other. Nothing more was said.

We understand each other perfectly, thought the Dragonslayer. I know she's the daughter of a king. She knows I know she's the daughter of a king. I know she knows I know . . . That's enough of that.

He laughed out loud and got a funny look from Jackie. There really must be something to this communication without words, he thought. Maybe Ron wasn't shy, just a bit ahead of his time. Centuries ahead even.

V

The Dragonslayer went to bed feeling quite good about the dragon and the future in general. This was, after all, what being a dragonslayer was all about.

He thought they should try to kill it in full view of the village, or at least where the villagers could inspect it afterwards. After so much fear, they deserved to see it killed, or at least dead. A nice carcass, very dead, would make them more generous, too, and not only with the formal payment.

That reminded him that he was meeting the mayor and councillors in the morning to sign a contract. He had already been warned that the deputy mayor, the man he had already met, was the real power in the village, and not only because he was the mayor's father-in-law. He had a reputation for being shrewd and rather ruthless about getting his own way. The Dragonslayer knew the type: not unlike dragons . . .

And with that thought, he fell asleep.

The following morning he inspected his preparations. The barriers were light, but probably strong enough to make the dragon use the open streets. The pits, which the villagers had dug quickly and efficiently exactly where he wanted them, were deep, had pointed shafts set upright in the bottom, and were covered with canvas and branches.

The dragon might be smart enough to avoid them — a black one certainly would be — but the idea was that it would either fall into one of the pits or have to pass between them. They could then attack it where it couldn't manoeuvre.

The Dragonslayer had hunters up the mountain watching for it and a system of signals to tell him when it was coming. In the village square he had the butcher ready to kill an ox. The smell of meat and blood would attract the dragon.

The villagers were warned to stay inside, but to watch what was happening. If the dragon attacked a house they should be able to get out without too much risk, if they kept their heads. Some wouldn't. He assured them that the dragon didn't really breathe fire, but of course he wasn't believed.

He intended that the dragon should come right into the square, where he would try to deal with it. If it stood its ground, Ron and Jackie would attack its rear. If it retreated, he hoped it would do so along the route he intended. First preference then was for the dragon to fall into one of the prepared pits. If it avoided them, it would have to either stand and fight or retreat between them. In either case, but preferably the latter, the Dragonslayer would attack and Ron and Jackie would again tackle it from the rear.

Hours passed and nothing happened. As always, the Dragonslayer found himself wishing for action. It always carried the risk of being killed or injured, but that never seemed as bad as just waiting around thinking about it.

The villagers began to get restless. Several appeared on the streets. The Dragonslayer warned them that the dragon was more likely to appear late in the day, answered their questions politely and gave them a direct order only if it was really necessary. A blue twilight descended on the village as the sun dropped behind a mountain, the highest eastern peaks were still brightly lit, high clouds were glowing pink . . . and everything happened at once.

The signal came from the mountain. Suddenly the dragon was in the village. It ran swiftly up the street toward the square as if it had never considered another route. The butcher hadn't had time to kill the ox. The Dragonslayer gave him the signal to go, and the butcher, plump and no longer young, ran faster than he had for years.

Professionally, the Dragonslayer noted that the data he had been given was accurate: Blue-green, male, about five metres long. Looked young, and was therefore big for its age. Fit, agile and aggressive. Probably no grasp of the danger armed humans presented. Willing to take on anything.

At least it isn't a black, he thought.

The dragon raced into the square, its eyes on the ox which was bellowing in terror and tugging at its rope. The dragon didn't pay any attention to the Dragonslayer until he spurred his horse to a full gallop. Then it swung to face him and drew its head back and up, the great frill behind its head standing out stiffly. Its wings were spread and its long neck was drawn back to strike. Its mouth opened, showing its fangs. Then it crouched and waited.

The Dragonslayer's tactics depended on his horse and its training. He charged directly at the dragon's head and at the last moment gave the horse a signal; the merest twitch of left rein, the lightest pressure of right leg. The horse swerved left and the Dragonslayer swung his sword backhanded at the point where the dragon's neck joined the skull. He missed. The dragon had reacted instantly to the horse's swerve and drawn its head back. The blade took it across the mouth. It screamed, reared up, crashed down and charged.

The horse wheeled, then sidestepped. The dragon followed its every move. The Dragonslayer revised his estimate of its experience. This one had faced a horseman before, and being here now meant that it had won. He stabbed at its neck. The dragon moved nimbly backward, enveloping him in a cloud of black vapour. Then it charged again. Behind it, he glimpsed Ron galloping up, Jackie behind him. He wanted to shout to her to keep away, that this was out of her class, but he had no time.

The dragon saw Ron and hurled itself at the Dragonslayer. The great head filled his field of vision for a few moments before another cloud of vapour obscured it. There was no time for a full stroke. He thrust, felt the sword hit bone and knew it had done little harm.

The dragon ignored it and swung its tail to the right. Ron was galloping up the dragon's right side, Jackie up its left. Its tail smashed against the legs of Ron's horse, bringing it crashing to ground. Ron's left leg shattered under the horse's weight. The dragon glanced briefly down its right flank, then resumed its attack on the Dragonslayer.

Jackie saw the neck at full extension and still curved to the right. With little conscious thought, she tightened her right rein and pressed inward with her left leg. The horse moved to the right and she slashed down with her sword. The blade passed between two vertebrae and the dragon dropped. The horse cleared the dragon's head and wheeled around as it was trained to do, almost unseating her. She wasn't used to that much initiative in a horse.

The dragon was thrashing on the ground and she couldn't see either the Dragonslayer or Ron because of the dust it was kicking up. She rode slowly around the creature at a safe distance, not at all sure that it was she who had brought it down, or that it was mortally wounded. She found the Dragonslayer trying to protect Ron from the lashing tail, but the violence of the death-throes was dimishing and movement soon stopped altogether.

Jackie and the Dragonslayer looked at each other. "What happened?" they asked together.

"The tail got Ron's horse," said the Dragonslayer. "He's unconscious and his leg looks broken. There may be other injuries. We need help to lift the horse and get him out. Did you kill the dragon?"

"I don't know," said Jackie. She was beginning to tremble. If this was dragonslaying, you could keep it.

The Dragonslayer walked around the dragon and found the wound in its neck. "Did you do this?" he asked Jackie.

She tried to answer and found that her teeth were

chattering. She suddenly felt very cold. The Dragonslayer caught her as she fell.

She woke up in bed with one of the village women sitting beside her. It was Mrs Chatwell, the woman who'd screamed for them to kill the dragon when they arrived. When Jackie sat up and tried to ask a question, the woman threw her arms around her neck and hugged and kissed her.

"You killed the dragon!" she said.

"Is Ron all right?" asked Jackie.

"You killed the dragon," the woman repeated. "It was the bravest thing I ever saw."

"Did they get Ron out from under the horse?"

"You charged right up to it and cut its head off," said the woman. "You killed it. It was the bravest thing I ever saw."

"Tell me what happened to Ron!"

"I knew you and your friends would kill it the moment I saw you. Such a tall, handsome gentleman. Such a strong young man. Such a beautiful girl. I said to my neighbour, that's old Mrs Guffy, I said, 'We're safe now,' I said. 'They'll kill the dragon, just you see if they don't', and you did. I knew you would. I said so. You rode straight up to it and cut its head off —"

"I don't think I actually cut its head off," said Jackie.

"— and it died. Mind you, I thought it would get you when you passed out like that. 'Loss of blood,' I said to my neighbour, that's young Mr Pugwash. 'Probably bit her,' I said, 'somewhere it doesn't show. She's probably bleeding to death right now, see if she isn't,' I said. But the Dragonslayer carried you in here . . . my he's strong, not that you're more than a wee slip of a thing. And we undressed you —"

"He undressed me?" asked Jackie, blushing.

"Well, he took your boots off. I did the rest. And you didn't have a mark on you, not that I could find. He's gone back to see about his young man. Such a good-looking young man. Such a pity he was injured. Never be the same again, I shouldn't wonder, crushed under the horse like that. Even if the dragon's tail didn't hit him. It can't be good for you, that sort of thing."

"No," said Jackie, "I don't suppose it is."

"Never thought I'd see the day. Saw it all from my front window. Grandstand view, like they say in the papers. Never thought I'd have one. The dragon came charging up, straight for that poor man. He didn't seem to know what to do, didn't even try to get out of its way —"

"He was trying to kill it," said Jackie. "He *is* a dragonslayer. Getting out of the way doesn't kill many dragons."

"— and I thought he was dead for sure. I couldn't see properly by then, the dragon was in the way. The young man had disappeared. Couldn't see him. Couldn't see his horse either —"

"They were together. He was riding it."

"— and I thought they were both dead. I thought you were *all* dead. Then you rode up calmly beside it and cut its head off."

"Not calmly, and I didn't cut its head off."

"Near enough," said the woman. "I saw the huge gash in its neck when I ran past after the tall man called me. All that blood. I thought I was going to faint, I really did. I said to old Mr Drilady, that's my neighbour across the road, I said, 'Oh, I do feel queer', but he was just standing staring at the blood and didn't look too good himself and I don't think he heard me."

Jackie swung her legs out of bed and stood up.

"Oh you mustn't," said the woman. "You're injured, you killed a dragon, you have to rest, you can't possibly get up."

"I am up," said Jackie. "Where are my clothes?"

"Please don't. What'll he say? He said I had to look after you."

"You have," said Jackie. "I'm going out now. I have to find out what happened to Ron. I'm all right, I really am. I'm not injured. I only fainted, you know."

"It's the stress, all that galloping and swinging swords and cutting heads off dragons," said the woman. "I don't know how you stand it."

"Better than I'm standing this," muttered Jackie, but the woman didn't hear. She dressed and went in search of the Dragonslayer and Ron, but she found herself so much of a heroine in the village that it was difficult to get directions. Everybody wanted to show her the way.

Eventually she reached the hospital, a pleasant cottage with six beds, four of them in one large room where the Dragonslayer and Ron were holding court. That is, the Dragonslayer was answering questions and Ron was sitting up in bed, smiling in a dazed sort of way and nodding occasionally. In reply to her anxious questions, the Dragonslayer explained that Ron's leg was broken in several places, but there were no other injuries. Ron looked at her, nodded, and made another speech.

"You did well," he said.

"That is the finest accolade you will ever receive," said the Dragonslayer. "It's only the second time I've heard Ron praise anyone." And it's only the tenth time I've heard him use more than two words at a time, he added to himself.

The mayor and deputy mayor came in and wanted to know if the village could have the carcass. It had been suggested that they could get it stuffed and mounted and set up permanently in the square to commemorate the occasion. It might even scare other dragons away.

"Or attract them," said the Dragonslayer, and they looked horrified.

"Well, we have plenty of time to decide about that, but perhaps up the mountain, on that big bluff, would be better," said the mayor.

"Perhaps not at all," said the deputy mayor, and the mayor looked crestfallen.

The Dragonslayer told them they could do what they

liked with the carcass; it was theirs to dispose of, as it said in the contract.

The deputy mayor looked for a moment as if he might have forgotten that, but he recovered quickly. "We just wanted to make sure," he explained, "that you don't have any plans. I'm sure we could find a use for the carcass. We could use the hide to upholster the seats in the council chamber and mount the head over the mayoral chair."

The mayor looked enchanted.

"The craft guild could make something ornamental out of the claws," the deputy mayor continued. "And the skeleton could be set up in the village museum."

"We don't have a museum," said the mayor.

"We will," said the deputy mayor.

The village turned on a party the following night. Even the hospital was opened to everyone so Ron wasn't left out. Several of the younger women found him very attractive. They didn't seem to notice that he didn't have much to say.

The Dragonslayer and Jackie stayed together and thoroughly enjoyed themselves. The Dragonslayer admired the way she handled young men. It was obvious that she was a sensation in the village. Having killed a dragon helps, he thought.

The following morning, tired but without a hangover, the Dragonslayer accepted payment at a formal ceremony in the council chambers, attended by everybody except Ron and the woman who was nursing him. Not everyone could get inside, but the mayor ordered the windows opened and then talked very loudly. The crowd outside seemed satisfied.

That evening the Dragonslayer discussed with Jackie their plans for the immediate future without Ron. It would be many weeks, probably months, before his leg was fully mended and he was fit to ride and work hard again.

"We could wait for him," he said, "but we wouldn't be earning anything while we did. The alternative is to rest for a few days, then travel on and look for work. If we pick up a third person somewhere I could put them on a short-term contract."

Jackie agreed with the alternative plan.

The next morning a pedlar came to see them. He travelled through the towns and villages of the region, selling an incredible range of goods from his pack.

"Deputy mayor thought you might be interested," he said abruptly.

"Yes?" said the Dragonslayer.

"Well, I mean, it's up to you, isn't it? All I can do is tell you."

"What?"

"About the man," said the pedlar.

"What man?"

"The one in the other village."

"What about him?"

"Looking for a job, isn't he."

"What sort of a job?"

"You know," said the pedlar.

"Actually, I don't," said the Dragonslayer.

The man looked astonished. "But you're the Dragonslayer," he said in a puzzled voice. "You and the girl killed the dragon, didn't you? Or she did. That's what they say."

"Yes," said the Dragonslayer, "we killed the dragon. But I still don't know what you're trying to tell me. Who is this man? What sort of job does he want? Where is he?"

The Dragonslayer had trouble getting answers out of

the man. Finally Jackie took over, realising that the pedlar would think he had to explain things in detail to a girl.

The man lived in a village over the mountains, the pedlar explained. He had been assistant to a dragon-slayer who had died and was looking for a new job. He hadn't had much luck, and yes, he probably would be interested in a short-term contract.

"What did the dragonslayer die of?" the Dragonslayer asked.

"Old age, I reckon."

That was good. Killed on the job would not have been.

"Does the man have much experience?"

"Reckon so. Doesn't talk about it much."

Also good.

"Is he likely to still be in the village?"

The pedlar nodded. "He's settled down with a local woman, a widow. Helps her farm. Needs money for new equipment and wants to go back to his old job for a while."

"And where is the village?" the Dragonslayer asked. If he could find it easily himself, he could leave Jackie to keep an eye on Ron.

The pedlar explained that there was only one trail, well marked and impossible to miss. It led over the High Pass. As an afterthought, he added that it was advisable to leave at 3 am.

"Why?" said the Dragonslayer.

"If you leave any later, you'll be caught on the High Pass at sunset."

"Is that bad?"

"Only if you want to survive."

It wasn't until the Dragonslayer was toiling up the slopes that he really appreciated what the man had meant. This was High Pass as in *very* High Pass. About 2500 metres high. Without proper gear or a fire, no one would survive a night in the open.

He reached the summit at about 5 pm, with just enough time to get down to the forest on the other side before sunset. A bitter wind was blowing and he was grateful for both the shelter of the trees and wood for a fire.

VI

He reached the village two days later, very tired.
Climbing, high altitudes and long journeys
alone did not seem to agree with him any more. He
stayed at the inn overnight and next morning inquired
for the man he wanted. The landlord knew him well.

"Seems a good man. Comes in a lot, but doesn't drink
too much," the landlord said. "There's them as thinks
he married Widow Matchem for her farm, but he seems
genuinely fond of her and he doesn't know too much
about farming anyway. Willing to learn, though. Asks
questions, listens to the answers. One or two of the
youngsters kidded him along at first, had him doing
some daft things, but he took it in good part. Caught on

quickly. Wants to bring the farm up to date. Talks about going off dragonslaying to earn money. Seems it's his trade. That what you want him for?"

"Yes," said the Dragonslayer. "That's my line."

"Thought so. You've got the look."

"What look is that?" said the Dragonslayer, but got no answer.

"Well, I guess you'll be wanting to find him," said the landlord. "He'll be working in the long field beside the road this morning. That's on a bit, opposite way to where you came in, just across the first creek."

The Dragonslayer thanked him and decided to walk, leaving his horse to recover from the climb over the pass. He found the man repairing a fence and, again, was immediately recognised as a dragonslayer.

"Used to work for one," the man said by way of explanation.

"Want to work for one again?" asked the Dragonslayer.

"My name's Bill," the man said, which didn't seem terribly relevant at that moment.

"Are you looking for a job?"

"Depends."

"On what?"

"Lots of things." Bill looked as if he was thinking.

Here it comes, thought the Dragonslayer. The money. But Bill surprised him.

"Do you use magic?" Bill asked.

"If appropriate."

"Meaning?"

"I use whatever method seems best," the Dragonslayer said, "and that usually means physical methods against animals and dragons."

"I don't believe in magic," said Bill flatly.

"Neither do I," said the Dragonslayer, "but it does seem to work against witches and warlocks. Mostly, I think, because they believe in it themselves."

"Maybe."

"Well, do you want a job?"

"Maybe," said Bill.

It didn't sound to the Dragonslayer as if Bill was being deliberately awkward; more as if they simply hadn't reached the important issues yet. "I pay well," he said.

"We'll discuss that if I decide to work for you," said Bill.

"What else do you need to know?"

"What's your set-up? What sort of staff do you have? What kind of work do you do? Do you have any current contracts? Why do you need me?"

Not disinterested at all, thought the Dragonslayer. "Well, we're a small outfit, just my assistant and an apprentice. She's new, but she's very prom —"

"She?"

"Yes." Bill didn't say anything, so the Dragonslayer continued. "Ron, that's my assistant, was injured when we killed a dragon in High Nurking —"

"So that was your lot. It was the girl that killed it."

"How did you know?"

"News travels fast in these parts. Even faster when it's important. They said it was a girl killed it. Seems like they were right."

"Have you ever worked with a girl?" asked the Dragonslayer.

"No, but if your girl killed a dragon she must be all right. What colour? Just a young one, was it?"

"Blue-green. Yes, it was young, but experienced. It had faced horsemen before."

"You can always tell," said Bill. "So it injured your assistant. And the girl's just started, has she?"

"Yes. She's an apprentice. New. Very promising."

"She killed the dragon," said Bill drily. "How come?" Meaning: *Where were you and what were you doing?*

The Dragonslayer realised that this wasn't someone to pitch a yarn to, so it was the truth or nothing.

"It knocked the legs from under Ron's horse with its tail," he said, "after covering me in a cloud of vapour. I was hitting it, but I knew I wasn't doing much harm. Ron and Jackie had both come up from behind. It got Ron, turned back to me and Jackie came up on its left side and put a sword cut neatly between two vertebrae."

"Luck?" asked Bill.

"I can only presume not. She's sixteen, led a fairly protected life until she walked out of it, has certainly had no relevant experience since, except that she's a fine rider and seems to know exactly what she's doing. She's got quite a sense of humour," he added, "and I think she's going to be excellent." He was surprised by his own words, and at the realisation that he meant it.

"And now?" asked Bill.

The Dragonslayer knew he was definitely going to join the team, provided a few final details were satisfactory.

"Contracts?" asked Bill.

"I'll offer you the usual terms, standard assistant's contract. Wages as per contract plus ten percent, with usual expenses and extras. Gear supplied or use your own on usual terms. Bonus to be decided by me if I consider a job well enough done. Everything signed up before you start, anything you're doubtful about thoroughly discussed and settled. Any special conditions written in, nothing left to argue about later."

"You worked with James Jackson years ago, didn't you?" said Bill. "Back before you were rated dragonslayer."

"That's right. Did you know him?"

"He was my uncle. I'll accept your offer."

"How soon can you start? I can wait a day or two, or if you need longer I'll head back and you can come later."

"I leave with you tomorrow morning. No need to hang around now I've decided. I'll explain to the wife over the meal tonight and meet you at the inn."

"Take longer if you need it."

"Don't," said Bill.

*

They left early the following morning. They maintained a comfortable pace and crossed the High Pass that afternoon, with plenty of time to find a good place to camp. Their riding horses were tired, even with all the gear on Bill's packhorse. Now that he had joined the team, Bill was a great deal more outgoing and talked about his earlier experience, which was extensive.

The Dragonslayer noted that whenever Bill spoke about a successful operation it was always "we", meaning the whole team, which had sometimes numbered as many as four. But when he was talking about his own mistakes it was always "I". The Dragonslayer liked him.

They rested for a full day, talking, discussing weapons and tactics, reminiscing and discussing great dragonslayers, past and present. The Dragonslayer was surprised at how many Bill had met at one time or another, and how often their views about them coincided.

They reached High Nurking early in the afternoon and found the village still excited about the killing of the dragon. The Dragonslayer was greeted warmly by everyone, and many introduced themselves to Bill, who smiled politely and said little. Ron was much improved and was taking a little exercise.

Jackie didn't seem to have missed the Dragonslayer. She had been organising the production of a play put on by the young people of the village, an ancient drama with several good parts and many small ones. The Dragonslayer watched part of a rehearsal and saw that it was going well. Opening night was three nights away.

"Can we stay for it?" asked Jackie. "I know we should be leaving and we do need to find a job, but I'd like to see how they do in performance. Please can we stay?"

"Of course," he said.

It was just as well they did. On the morning of the performance, a young man arrived on a tired horse and took a room at the inn. A few minutes later he came rushing out looking for the Dragonslayer.

"Are you really a dragonslayer?" he said when he found him. "I mean, they say you killed a dragon here, but is it your job? I mean, do you do it professionally? Can you help us? We'll pay well. But we have to have someone who really knows what they're doing. We've had so many people killed trying to kill them. They're so strong and so fast, and attack from above and —"

"I think you'd better slow down and start from the beginning," said the Dragonslayer.

"Right." The young man took a deep breath.

His name was Jack and he came from Bridgeford, a market town many miles to the south. And they did need a dragonslayer, badly.

The threat was from a pair of giant birds, rare now but by no means unheard of. They were a mated pair, hunting together, more than big enough to carry off children and small animals, and to kill large ones. And they had done so, many times. The whole district was desperate. Repeated attempts had been made to kill the birds, or drive them away, but all that had happened was that more and more people had been killed. Including the messenger's father.

Jackie, who had been listening closely, looked at Jack with sudden sympathy. His hysteria and intense manner were no longer funny. The beast they had captured at Westhaven hadn't killed anybody. Even the two people killed at Nigh Nurking hadn't had any relatives. But here was a young man whose father had been killed by the creatures they were being called on to dispose of: giant birds. She wasn't sure that she liked the idea of giant birds. Then she remembered that she hadn't liked the idea of the dragon either, when she saw how it had terrified the village. But she had coped in the event, even if not as well as everyone seemed to think.

The Dragonslayer suddenly realised that Jack was on his last legs. "When did you last eat?" he asked.

Jack didn't seem to know. "Yesterday, or maybe the day before," he said vaguely. The Dragonslayer suspected that it was longer than that.

Jack admitted that he hadn't thought about anything but reaching High Nurking after hearing a rumour at another village about a dragonslayer being in those parts. That village was three days' ride away, but Jack had done it in two. The Dragonslayer persuaded Jack to go back to the inn for a meal and a sleep and promised to talk with him later.

When Jack woke up several hours later, he looked better and was much more coherent. His story was a chilling one, not least because he had actually seen his father killed.

Bridgeford was a market town in a big, closely-farmed

river valley many days' travel away. The birds had appeared in the valley three years earlier. They were big even then, but apparently no great threat. No one worried because they preyed on rabbits.

They had grown frighteningly fast. The previous year they had attacked a man in the hills, who had escaped only by diving from a high cliff into the river. He had been lucky to survive both the birds and the escape. People had rationalised that he must have been near their nest, and hoped for the best.

They had been disappointed. After a summer of missing lambs and calves, and two more attacks on people — not serious because they had been able to get to shelter quickly — the birds had disappeared at the start of winter. Everyone had heaved a sigh of relief. But with spring they had come back, much bigger, and now they could tackle any living thing in the valley and kill it.

"Are you sure they're the same birds?" asked the Dragonslayer.

"Definitely," said Jack. They had distinctive marks, including some resulting from the attempts to kill them. Despite the townspeople's earlier thoughts, they didn't appear to have nested.

"No," the Dragonslayer agreed, "they'd be too young yet."

"Do you know what they are? Can you kill them?" asked Jack, becoming agitated again.

"Yes, I do know what they are," the Dragonslayer said. "Expect them to grow much bigger."

Jack paled.

"Two are worse than one," the Dragonslayer continued, "much worse in fact, because they hunt and fight as a team. The attempts to kill this pair have probably ensured that they're very highly skilled indeed."

The early countermeasures had almost succeeded, Jack explained, but the later ones had been increasingly dangerous.

The Dragonslayer had killed two single, very similar birds, one quite early in his career. He had never tackled a pair, though his father had, and had always described it as one of his more difficult contracts.

"Can you help us?" Jack pleaded. "More than twenty people have been killed. We can't go on like this. They're picking us off. Not to mention our livestock. Some farmers have just about been wiped out."

The Dragonslayer looked grave. He had had no idea

that anything like twenty people had been killed by the birds. That was serious. Even a dragon seldom killed that many, if only because the people usually just fled the district.

He questioned Jack about the methods that had been used to try to kill the birds, and didn't like what he heard. After some half-baked, mostly single-handed attempts that had failed badly, the citizens had organised themselves and gone about it in a highly intelligent, military manner. They had tried several of the methods the Dragonslayer would have considered, and by Jack's account had carried them out well.

And that, of course, had given the birds valuable experience and training. Like the dragon at High Nurking, they had faced armed, organised humans and won. They had obviously learned and remembered, or they wouldn't have survived the steadily improving attacks the citizenry had mounted against them and be able to continue killing their attackers.

"Yes, we'll come," the Dragonslayer assured Jack, hoping that Jackie and Bill would agree. Although he could overrule them, he preferred to operate by majority decision. As his father had always said, "The semblance of democracy is better than democracy, provided the resemblance is close enough . . ."

"When?" asked Jack.

"Tomorrow morning," said the Dragonslayer, hoping a reputation for being quick off the mark wouldn't be ruined by Jack discovering that they had planned to leave then anyway.

Jack visibly relaxed.

Jackie invited him to the play that night. He seemed to enjoy the first act, but then fell asleep.

The Dragonslayer watched with his mind on other things. He had some experience of giant birds, though not really big ones like these ones Jack was talking about. He knew quite a bit about them, because they could be very difficult, and dragonslayers tended to talk about them a great deal. Two of them — big, hunting as a pair and now experienced in dealing with hostile humans — was very bad news indeed.

He would have to warn Jackie that this job would probably be far more difficult and far more dangerous than the dragon. She had done exceptionally well in killing it, but she must also have known that there had been a considerable element of good luck. There would be no room for luck with these birds. With them, it would be either efficiency and success, or disaster.

During the interval he had a quick word with Bill, who shared his appreciation of the danger. The Dragonslayer spent the rest of the play deciding what he would tell Jackie. It was important not to frighten her, but even more important to make sure that she understood what they were getting into.

He called Jackie and Bill to a brief meeting before they went to bed. Without revealing that he and Bill had spoken privately earlier, he stressed that the birds were very dangerous, that careful planning, meticulous execution and tight discipline would be essential. Jackie said she understood, and went off to bed looking very thoughtful.

The next morning they left for Bridgeford with Jack.

VII

Jack was rested, fed and much more relaxed. He was good company, and he got on well with Jackie and Bill.

The first stage of the journey, over a high pass, was difficult. The pass wasn't as high as the one between High Nurking and Bill's village, but the track was both rougher and steeper, and much less used. Once they were over the pass the going became easier, the grades less steep and the passes less high. Much of their travel was through river valleys and quite easy. Small villages were frequent, and food and accommodation were no problem.

Some of the villages seemed remote and primitive,

and Jackie began to refer to High Nurking as the Mountain Metropolis, but eventually the villages grew bigger, and more sophisticated.

They began to hear about the giant birds, which had occasionally foraged this far afield and been seen in the sky. They also heard some stories that Bill said were greatly exaggerated. But there'd been further deaths in the valley, and that worried him.

Two days later Jack led them off the road to the east and directly toward the mountains. He said Bridgeford was in the next valley, though many kilometres downstream from where they would enter it. They would cross the mountains over a low cwm.

"Over a low what?" asked Jackie.

He spelt it, but Jackie was still puzzled.

It seemed that cwm was a dialect word, and that he meant what Jackie would have called a saddle and the Dragonslayer a col.

"You'll probably find a lot of words like that in the valley," Jack told them. "We do a lot of things our way, or so outsiders tell us."

"I grew up speaking a patois no one outside my own village could understand," the Dragonslayer told him.

"I can never remember much of it these days, but if I run into anyone who speaks it, it all comes back."

As they rode up a small valley toward the steep trail at its head, they came clear of a small wood. Jack reined in and signalled for them to stop and be quiet.

"Look," he whispered and pointed across the fields to their left. At first they didn't see anything untoward. Then they noticed a cattle beast that was acting strangely, tossing its head and pawing the ground; turning away, then back, then repeating the whole performance.

"Why is it doing that?" Jackie asked.

"See where it's looking?" Jack said.

She looked, and saw her first giant bird. It sat on the ground, tall and alert but still, staring at the cattle beast.

"What's happening? Why doesn't it attack if it's going to?"

Jack glanced at the sky. "Watch the cattle beast."

A moment later a black cloud fell from the sky and enveloped the cattle beast. It was seconds before Jackie realised that it was a second bird, and by that time the animal was down and the bird was tearing at its throat. Its mate took off with a single powerful beat of its wings, then glided to join it. Together, they began to dismember the carcass and a few moments later they took off, each gripping about a quarter of the beast in its talons. Jackie shuddered.

"That was brilliant," she muttered. "How could they attack as intelligently as that? The first one made the beast watch it, but didn't attack. Then the second one, that the beast didn't know was there, took it out."

"That's right," said Jack. "If the first one had got too close and spooked it, the beast would've run for the trees and probably made it. The birds know exactly what they're doing. Sometimes they 'stoop' — drop from the sky — without the double act, but often the prey sees the shadow and takes off. They have to do it that way when they hunt alone but when they're together you usually see the double act — or the start of it, if you're lucky."

"Lucky?" said Jackie.

"If ever you see one on the ground just watching you, remember that the second one's above you and coming fast. Turn right round and run. Head for the nearest cover, even a wall or fence, anything that can stop the bird dropping on to you. Remember, it won't want to hit anything hard or sharp if it's dropping fast." He grinned. "It's like the old joke: If you're confronted by a dangerous animal, what steps should you take? Answer: Very many fast ones."

"Why turn round?" Bill asked. "Wouldn't it be faster to take off the way you're facing?"

"Yes, but the bird in the air will be facing its mate as it drops, and if you run straight ahead it'll open its wings and glide after you. Then you'll be getting closer to the one on the ground, and that's not a good idea. But if you turn and run, the dropping bird has to do a longer manoeuvre and you'll have a better chance of getting away. A *slightly* better chance. But when you see a bird on the ground, don't stop and stare. If you do, the bird may be the last thing you see."

The Dragonslayer said nothing. He knew that the performance they had just seen was fairly standard. The birds hunted at a great height, well separated but in sight of each other. When one bird spotted prey or potential prey, it either attacked straight away or started the sequence they had just seen. The other bird would then come in to make the kill.

Jackie became very thoughtful. She recalled her initial fear at High Nurking, but at least a dragon attacked on the ground. Suddenly dragons didn't seem so terrible compared to something that might drop out of the sky without warning.

"They've attacked humans," Jack said, "but only if they're on their own. If they're on horseback they go for the person, not the horse. And then the second bird attacks the horse. But if there's more than one mounted human, they stay clear."

Jackie felt relieved.

Then Jack spoiled it by saying, "But there's always a first time, I suppose."

"The birds have disappeared," Bill pointed out. "I suppose they came over the mountains because food's getting scarce, or because it's too well protected in the valley."

"Possibly," said Jack, "but they foraged outside the valley before, even when there was still food there. They're more than smart enough not to clear out the supplies in one place."

"That's true," said the Dragonslayer. "I haven't had much experience with giant birds, but the way they're acting fits with everything I've heard. The decoy tactic is standard, and so is the wide foraging. Sometimes it's taken a long time to find their nest or roosting place when they're in the wilderness."

The Dragonslayer sighed and turned to Jack. "This might be a good time to tell you, Jack, that although I don't blame your people for trying to kill them, it's actually made the situation worse. Some of the methods they used were very good, but in effect those methods have *trained* the birds. Very well. They can probably cope with any tactics we use now."

"You didn't have to cope with them killing your stock, or your friends and relatives," Jack said.

"I know," said the Dragonslayer. "I wasn't criticising. But these birds are going to be very difficult, and nothing that's happened to date has helped. I don't know if any of you noticed, but the whole time the birds were butchering that carcass they kept a close watch on us, and they gave us a wide berth when they took off. They're very smart indeed. This isn't going to be easy."

"Do you know how we're going to tackle them?" asked Jackie.

"Not specifically," said the Dragonslayer, "though I have several possibilities in mind." He wasn't bluffing. He had been giving the matter a great deal of thought.

"I'll need to find out exactly what's been done and try to come up with a new strategy, preferably something not only new to them but something that none of the experience they've had so far will help them counter. That may not be easy."

They started the steep climb out of the valley and conversation lapsed as their horses tackled the narrow trail. It took almost an hour to reach the top, where they paused and looked down at the sluggish river flowing through the broad valley. There was no stock in sight. The valley was very fertile, and some fields looked particularly lush because the grass was not being grazed. Many were mown, and men were working in others. Jack explained that the grass was being cut and fed to the stock indoors. There were a number of crops, which looked well-tended. But nowhere was there anyone working alone. There were a number of armed lookouts.

It took them only thirty-five minutes to reach the valley floor. They rode downstream until they reached a bridge, then crossed and picked up a main highway on the far side of the valley. After that, it would be a full day's journey to Bridgeford.

An hour later they met a group of mounted people riding the other way. They stopped to talk.

"The attacks are getting worse," one of the riders said. "Two more people have been killed." One had been a lone horseman, the other a farmer who had tried to protect an animal. The bird stooping from the sky had switched from the cow to him and killed him. In sight of his family.

Jackie shivered.

The riders were polite, but subdued. Jackie had the feeling that they no longer expected very much. The birds had become a fixture in their lives.

They spent the night at an inn in a small village. It was clean, comfortable and the food was good. The inn keeper was almost pathetically grateful to see them.

"Very few people travelling now," he said. "Too frightened, even though they're safe in company. And it's not only that. Commerce has slowed almost to a stop. No stock trading, of course."

He explained that nobody dared move cattle or sheep on the roads, although no mob or herd escorted by mounted riders had been attacked. But clearly the birds were killing the valley, mainly in less obvious ways than by killing stock and people. They were bringing everything to a standstill, and it couldn't go on.

"You going to do something about them?" he said to the Dragonslayer.

Like most people, he had recognised the Dragonslayer instantly for what he was.

"We're here to do our best," the Dragonslayer said. "They're going to be very difficult, and frankly, I don't guarantee success. But we'll do our best."

"Yes, well, I guess that's all we can expect. Do our best. That's all any of us can do, isn't it? Our best. Can't ask more than that, can we?" The inn keeper wasn't impressed and made little effort to conceal it. But he remained friendly and wished them well, rather half-heartedly, when they left the following morning.

They had a long day on the road, passing very few people, and those they did see were all in groups. Fields were being worked, but never by only one or two people and with armed lookouts very much in evidence.

They reached Bridgeford after dark and Jack saw them settled at an inn before going to his own home. He said he would see the town manager that night and arrange for them to meet him the following morning.

"It's likely to be early, say seven-thirty," he said. "Will that be OK? He's always at his desk by seven and he doesn't waste time."

The Dragonslayer assured him that seven-thirty would be fine. Actually, he liked the sound of that. It suggested efficiency, though nothing would substitute for actually meeting the man, whose name he learned was Harry Jackson. He inquired about other officials.

Jack told him there would be none to worry about at this stage. The manager had been put in sole charge of all matters relating to the birds quite early. "The town council and senior staff thought it would be more efficient," he explained.

The Dragonslayer wondered if they had thought of that for themselves, or if the early-rising Mr Jackson had planted the idea. Some lines from an old poem ran through his head: *In seasons of great peril / 'Tis good that one bear sway; / Then choose we a Dictator, / Whom all men shall obey*. It had been good advice two thousand years ago, and it would be the same today, if the man chosen was up to the job. He went to bed and slept well.

MAYOR
JACKSON

BIRD FILE

VIII

They were up bright and early the following morning, and Jack arrived just after seven to escort them to manager Jackson's office. The town hall was an old stone building, tasteful and well-maintained. Neat lawns and colourful gardens surrounded it. The manager's office was on the first floor: large, bright, airy and uncluttered.

Harry Jackson rose from his desk and came to greet them as soon as they entered. He was relaxed and informal and got down to business straight away. Without waiting to be asked, he produced a thick file on the birds. It was well indexed.

The Dragonslayer noted at a glance that the birds had

been kept under almost constant observation for a long time. Feeding habits, flight patterns, choice of food, times. It had all had been carefully noted.

"We can predict where they will be, and when, with reasonable accuracy," the manager told them. "Since we sent Jack to find a dragonslayer, I've made sure they haven't been disturbed. Let them settle into a routine, as much as possible. I realise that some of our early attempts to deal with them ourselves were amateurish. I think we did a bit better later, but we still didn't succeed. I accept that we've done more harm than good, though not *too* much harm, I hope."

While they talked, people were coming and going; asking a question, receiving an answer, sometimes handing him a paper. Most he just glanced at before signing, but some he read, first asking his visitors' permission. Occasionally he touched a bell and asked whoever answered it to do something, and sometimes he made a request to one of the callers that had nothing to do with the matter that person had raised.

When the Dragonslayer inquired about specific points, Harry Jackson always had facts and figures at his fingertips. The Dragonslayer was impressed. "I'll take the file away and study it," he said, and was about to ask for maps when the manager handed him another folder, saying simply, "Maps."

"I'll study the file today," the Dragonslayer said, "and get back to you as soon as I have some ideas. I'll need your expertise and local knowledge to tell me what's possible in terms of terrain and resources, including people."

"Right," said the manager. "I'll hear from you when you're ready."

"Doesn't seem a very forceful character," Jackie said as they left the town hall. She wasn't impressed.

"Don't you think so?" said the Dragonslayer. "Did you notice that while we were there he never issued a single order; that he made many courteous requests that were instantly obeyed. That's the mark of a man in total control of himself, his job and his staff. I imagine kings act that way. Good ones, anyway."

Jackie looked startled for a moment, then agreed.

The Dragonslayer smiled to himself. There was no harm in letting her know that he hadn't forgotten what they both knew.

By late afternoon the Dragonslayer was ready to talk

to the manager again. Jackie and Bill waited outside.

"I have senior staff standing by," the manager said. "I suggest we have a general discussion first so that I can decide who we need, then we can get down to details as a group, keeping it as small as possible. Suit you?"

The Dragonslayer nodded. He briefly outlined half a dozen ideas. Jackson ruled out two immediately. There was no suitable terrain within easy reach for the first, and no technical resources for the second. The other four were entirely practicable. Jackson suggested that he call in the appropriate experts.

Four senior staff officers joined them and were briefly introduced. The Dragonslayer noticed a distinct lack of the pretentious titles and ridiculously formal procedures that had marked the Westhaven council. They all met as equals and what they said was always to the point. They discussed each other's specialties without regard to boundaries of responsibility or other protocols. It was an efficient, productive business meeting and the Dragonslayer knew that only the birds would create problems; he would have none with these people. He also knew which plan he was going to attempt first.

With planning, skill and discipline, and perhaps a little luck, it would be the only plan he would need.

"I think that covers everything we need to know at this stage," he said. "I'll discuss the options with my staff and decide which one we'll try first. I'll be back here early tomorrow and we can get down to detailed planning."

He walked back to the inn with Jackie and Bill. "Notice how we haven't once been asked to hurry up and get on with it?" he said. "Very professional, these people, and they treat us the same way."

At their inn, they were given a private room for a conference, with food and drink provided, and the Dragonslayer set about getting Jackie and Bill to prefer the plan he had already decided was best.

He started by outlining the advantages and disadvantages of each of the four plans, moving on to the next the moment Jackie and Bill showed any enthusiasm for his choice. By the time he had dealt with all four, they were clamouring for closer consideration of the plan he wanted and, with a show of reluctance, he allowed himself to be persuaded.

With a firm decision made, they got down to detailed

planning: deciding how many weapons would be necessary, what was essential at the killing ground, what personnel were needed over and above the men with weapons, what should be done immediately, and how long it would   take to set up once the weapons were available. It took several hours to work out all the details and when they had finished all three were ready for bed.

They were back with Jackson and his staff early the following morning.

"We've decided on the massed weapons plan," the Dragonslayer told them. "There are three other options if it fails, but if everyone makes the right effort with this one, we won't need the others. Mr Jackson assures me that mass production of the weapons is not a problem, but there are one or two matters that could be put in hand at once. Do we need to consult with village councils, farmers' organisations or others?"

"No," said Jackson. "As soon as we decided to send for a dragonslayer we got the authority of every affected body in the valley."

They also had regional authority within the valley to enforce decisions, and impose severe penalties on failure to comply with directives. There had been some opposition, of course, but most people realised that the birds had to be dealt with and were prepared to put up with whatever was necessary to get rid of them.

Jackson had spoken with some bitterness, and the Dragonslayer realised that getting such a free hand to deal with the birds hadn't been as simple as he made it sound.

"We'll try to cause as little disruption as possible," the Dragonslayer said, "but we can't afford to skimp on the plan. The first thing is to get the birds hungry, or at least get them flying a long way to find food. Then they'll be more ready to take food from us when we offer it. I realise that people are already taking extreme care to protect themselves and their stock, but I want everyone to try to make sure that the birds don't feed. I don't want anyone taking stupid risks, but they should try to scare away any wild animals, such as rabbits. I want the birds hungry and tired of foraging by the time we're ready to deal with them."

Jackson made no comment. He called in a staff member and gave him simple, concise instructions. It was as close to a direct order as the Dragonslayer had heard him give.

"Now to weapons," the Dragonslayer continued to the men assembled in front of him. "The plan is to entice the birds within range and kill them with a volley from massed crossbows. To do that, we have to have the crossbows. I know there are a number of hunting weapons available, but we need many more, and they need to shoot a much heavier bolt than is used in hunting. Mr Jackson tells me that enough metal- and woodworking workshops are available to produce what we need quickly. Here are the specifications my staff and I drew up last night." He turned to Jackson. "Do we need to talk to the people who'll be doing the work?"

"No," said Jackson. "The heads of the wood- and metalworking guilds are on standby. With these specifications, we can prepare detailed duplicate plans and distribute them to individual workshops."

He assured the Dragonslayer that the two hundred crossbows needed could be built in a fortnight at the most, probably less, if the parts of all weapons did not have to be interchangeable with each other.

"I assumed that for what is essentially a one-off job, that wouldn't be necessary," said the manager. "It would be a different matter if we were going to fight a prolonged campaign and had to repair weapons in the field. That's correct, I take it?"

"Perfectly," said the Dragonslayer, and his regard for Jackson's professionalism went up another notch.

"I also asked about bolts," said the manager. "I suggested as a starting point that three per crossbow would be enough. It seems unlikely that there'll be a chance for more than three volleys. They see no problem with producing them at the same time as the crossbows. They'll all be available together."

"Fine," said the Dragonslayer.

The manager gave an assistant the crossbow specifications and asked him to get them duplicated and given to the guild heads. "What next?" he asked.

"People," said the Dragonslayer. "Firstly, the crossbowmen. We need two hundred men who know how to handle a crossbow."

"We don't have more than a hundred and fifty, and some of them aren't very expert," said Jackson. "Mostly a volunteer militia unit, which is no more than a hobby for most of them, and the rest professional hunters and some good amateurs. The professional hunters will be the best marksmen."

"That's better than I expected," said the Dragonslayer. It wasn't, but there was no point in saying so. "As soon as the first weapons become available, we start training another fifty men. They won't have to be too expert. The whole point of the plan is the massed volley. A man who aims at a sitting bird and misses might put a bolt through its neck as it takes off. We'll use the best marksmen as back-up, the men who, we hope, will dispose of a wounded bird as it tries to escape. Who can we put in charge of recruiting and training?"

"The colonel of the militia," said the manager. Seeing the Dragonslayer raise his eyebrows at "colonel", he added, "It's a pretentious title, but a traditional one. He's good. The militia, for all that the men are part-time and amateurs, are fit and disciplined. We use them a lot in emergencies and special situations. It's just that crossbows aren't their preferred weapon. I've told the colonel that he and his men will be needed, and I've outlined some possibilities, including this one. You can talk to him as soon as we finish here. I'll have him told what you need now, and by the time you meet him he'll have some concrete ideas to discuss."

"Fine," said the Dragonslayer again.

They went on to discuss catering for the men in the field, and the provision of medical and other necessary services. It was a major undertaking, and needed to be planned very carefully. Two hundred armed men were going to be in a confined space, certainly for several days and possibly for much longer. It was going to be crowded and uncomfortable and the first priorty was not to scare the birds off. Nothing could be left to chance.

Finally, everything was sorted out and passed on to a specific person who had the responsibility for the job and the authority to do it. Then they got down to the question of where they were going to set their trap: the killing ground.

The council executives had obviously been briefed about that also and had a number of suggestions. What was needed was a large open space surrounded by trees. The canopy had to be dense enough to hide men on the ground, and marksmen in the upper branches.

Two of the sites sounded ideal. The Dragonslayer and his team went with the men to inspect them. The Dragonslayer chose the one most distant from the town as the one more likely to be attractive to the birds. In the clearing he went over the plan in detail with Jackson and his men.

"I want most of the crossbowmen — all except the marksmen — spread around the clearing, just inside the trees. Breastworks will have to be built to protect them from stray bolts, fired from the far side. It's a pity the clearing isn't wider than the range of a crossbow."

"If it were," said the manager, "you'd need far more men. For the bigger perimeter."

"Er, yes," said the Dragonslayer, who hadn't thought of that. He went on hurriedly. "I want a number of cattle among the trees to disguise the sound and smell of humans."

The manager gave instructions, then turned back to the Dragonslayer. "The men will stay in position as long as necessary. Coming and going must be kept to a minimum; we don't know what may alert the birds. All supplies will come in at night. No fires, no noise. Nothing that may give away the presence of humans."

He pointed to a group of men with shovels, who had just arrived in the clearing. "I've arranged for latrines to be sited and dug. Further back there will be ten places from which meals will be distributed."

"Very well," said the Dragonslayer, mentally crossing those items off his list. This man was efficient in a *big* way, he thought.

Jackson continued. "Some of the cattle will be let out into the clearing as bait for the birds." He turned to one of his men. "Organise it," he said.

"There are some smaller clearings in the forest nearby," said the Dragonslayer. "I want some marksmen there, others in the treetops. Platforms or hides may have to be built."

The manager called another man over. "Positions for marksmen in treetops. Consult with the colonel of the militia, decide how many and where and get them built. You'll have to strike a balance between keeping them well concealed and allowing the marksmen a clear field of fire."

The man started to leave, but the Dragonslayer called him back. "I'll need some marksmen in the tallest trees beside this clearing where they can fire down at the birds on the ground."

"Right," said the man and hurried off.

Maybe three minutes to organise what would have taken three hours at Westhaven, thought the

Dragonslayer. And it will be done properly. He smiled.

"The crossbowmen will ring the clearing, but will be organised in small squads under the command of officers," he said. "They mustn't shoot until they get the order. If we drop the birds on the ground, fine; if not, it's up to the marksmen. We'll have a system of calls worked out to indicate which way they're going if they escape the bowmen."

Jackson and the Dragonslayer walked in silence together for several minutes while the Dragonslayer reviewed everything in his head. Unable to think of anything he had overlooked, he summarised the plan and emphasised the important points.

"The plan is simple to execute. It's designed for men with minimum skill, numbers making up for finesse. But it depends on discipline. There must be no fires, no noise, and nobody seen in the open. Above all, they must not shoot before they get the order. They must obey all orders. This must be stressed. If everyone plays their part, the plan will work."

"I'll give them a pep talk," said the manager.

They returned to town, where the Dragonslayer had a long discussion with the militia colonel, whose own planning was well advanced. He was an accountant, but had already demonstrated a good knowledge of military history, a clear mind and an ability to organise totally at odds with his nondescript appearance. He made some comments about the strategic genius of Alphonse IV in the Wars of the Disputed Succession, which delighted Jackie and caused the Dragonslayer to conclude that she was probably the famous king's great-granddaughter. Not that that was any help in identifying her, he thought. Alphonse, in addition to being a military genius, had fathered a huge family and most of the royal house of the United Kingdoms included his descendants.

The Dragonslayer looked over to where Jackie was talking quietly with Bill. It would explain a lot about her, he thought.

IX

Less than a fortnight later, everything had been done as the Dragonslayer had requested and they were ready to go.

Before they took up their positions at the killing ground, he spoke to the crossbowmen and their officers. He went through the plan in detail, although he knew they were already familiar with it. He pointed out that no battle plan ever survived contact with the enemy, but that success was assured if everyone followed orders. He wasn't as confident as he sounded, but he took care not to show it.

"Now," he said, starting on what the men were likely to regard as the most important part of the proceedings, "you've been assigned to squads, and to fixed positions in those squads, and given a three-part number which indicates your squad, rank, and position in that rank. You each have your three crossbow bolts. What I want you to do as soon as you're in position under the trees is to carve your number on the shaft of each bolt, one to ten as the case may be for your squad, one to three for your rank, and one to seven for your own number. Use Roman numerals because they can be cut with straight lines. Don't make an artwork out of it, and above all, don't weaken the shaft of the bolt. All that's necessary is that we be able to identify every bolt that lodges in a bird. There'll be a substantial reward for the men who fired them."

The crossbowmen cheered.

They spent most of the night getting men into the forest, positioned around the clearing and settled down. The cattle, which were already there, were upset and noisy and the men didn't get much sleep.

The following day the final details were attended to, the marksmen sent to their platforms in the trees and the first cattle put out to graze in the clearing. The waiting began.

The men were in good spirits, many of them boasting about how they were going to get all three of their bolts into a bird before it knew what had struck it. The Dragonslayer knew this wouldn't last. Two or three days and boredom would set in, when it would become hard to keep the men still and quiet. A week, and it would be hard to keep some of them on the job at all.

He made an occasional round of the squads, talking to many of the men and asking them about their families and jobs. He encouraged Jack to do it occasionally and told Jackie not to. Her turn would come later. He didn't want to tell her that her principal role would be as a counter to boredom, although her ability to talk easily to people would be just as important as the fact that she was an attractive young woman, and the only one most of the men would actually see until the operation was over. The women who brought in food and other supplies at night would have little contact with the men.

There was a burst of excitement on the second day when one of the birds was seen high overhead, but it took no interest in the clearing and passed out of sight. When nothing happened for three more days, the problems began.

After discussions with the militia colonel, the Dragonslayer agreed that the men would have to be able to walk around, but only in small numbers at a given time, and with the permission of their officers. If there was an alert, they were to stop where they were and go to action stations with whatever unit they were closest to. He didn't want men dashing madly back to join their own squad and alerting the birds with noise and movement.

A few of the men were beginning to criticise the plan, saying it was a stupid idea and would never work. They suggested alternatives that had already been tried, ignoring the fact that they had failed and had in some cases resulted in people being killed. After another discussion with the colonel, the worst offenders were quietly sent home. The Dragonslayer half-remembered a line about those who spread bad morale being better dead, but couldn't quite put his finger on it.

Two days later the lookouts again sighted a bird, and the Dragonslayer barely had time to react before it appeared in the clearing. Most of the cattle bolted, but two, a bull and a cow with a slightly wild nature, stood their ground.

"Perfect," he breathed to himself. He hoped no one would make a noise, do anything stupid and, above all, would not try to be a hero by shooting at the bird before its mate arrived.

The wait seemed interminable.

When he had given up hope of the other bird attacking, there was a startled bellow from the bull and the sound of it bolting. The second bird had stooped on the cow.

"Shoot!"

The call came from the officers like a single voice, and the crossbows crashed almost as one. The bird that had felled the bull dropped, riddled with more bolts that the Dragonslayer could count at a glance. The other had leapt into the air just as the men fired and most of the bolts had missed. Two had hit, however, one through its crop where it was not likely to do much immediate harm, and the other through the wing near its body. The wing was at full upward extension, and the bolt had passed through from the underside and stuck there. The bolt protruding from the underside of its wing made it impossible for it to make a downstroke, necessary for flight.

Screaming like a banshee, it was struggling for altitude. At treetop height another bolt, this time from one of the marksmen in the trees, hit it mid-thigh. It faltered and lost a few metres in height, then struggled up again. It stopped screaming.

The officers called in its position and course to the marksmen. It was barely out of sight before the crash of crossbows, triumphant yells and the sound of a heavy body falling through branches announced that the bird was down.

After it was all over the Dragonslayer sat down against a tree, immensely relieved. It had gone like a text-book exercise. Both birds dead, no one killed, and only one man injured: one of the marksmen had been so keen to get down to see the dead bird that he had lost his footing and fallen, breaking a leg.

The Dragonslayer allowed the men the best part of an hour to inspect both birds and tell each other exactly what they had been doing when the first one appeared; how they had stood firm and shot only when ordered. Then he called them into the clearing, climbed into the lower branches of a tree and addressed them.

"Congratulations," he told them. "A first-class,

professional performance. You're the best I've ever worked with. We've collected the bolts out of the birds and the men who fired them will get their reward."

One of the men had been caught trying to push one of his bolts into a bird when he thought no one was watching. He had been soundly thumped by his mates and the Dragonslayer decided to take no further action, a decision with which the militia colonel later agreed.

The men made litters, loaded them with the fallen birds and equipment and began a triumphant march back into town, the birds at the head of the column. Word went ahead of them and they were met by a cheering crowd who escorted them to the town square.

The town dignitaries had been assembled under the cool eye of Harry Jackson, who had to let the mayor have his say on this occasion.

The mayor was brief and to the point. He thanked the Dragonslayer and his crew, thanked the town manager and all who had assisted in "this glorious enterprise", told the crossbowmen they were all heroes whose names would not soon be forgotten, and said the agreed fee would, of course, be paid in full, plus a bonus fifty percent greater than agreed on. This was official.

Unofficially, he understood a collection was already being taken up to allow individual townspeople to show their appreciation, and the Dragonslayer and his crew would also get that.

The Dragonslayer thanked the mayor. The crowd cheered. He said the men had been the best he had ever worked with. The crowd cheered. He then had the militia colonel call out the names of the men whose bolts had lodged in the birds. The crowd cheered and cheered. They cheered each of the men individually. All twenty-seven of them.

Then the feasting began.

X

It took them a long time to get away from Bridgeford. Once again they were treated as celebrities, but this time there were far more people wanting to entertain them. They didn't have to pay for a thing.

The Dragonslayer was prepared to let everyone, himself included, have a long break. The journey to Bridgeford had been a hard one and they had moved at a good pace the whole time. And he, especially, had found the strain of setting up and overseeing the massive plan to deal with the birds quite tiring.

When they did leave, more than a week later, they found it just as hard to make progress through the valley.

Word went ahead of them and the roads were lined with people. They had to stop and talk and accept hospitality at such frequent intervals that they took hours to cover a few kilometres. Late one night they reached the inn they had stayed at on their way to Bridgeford. The innkeeper greeted them like old friends and was genuinely delighted to see them, but he was also slightly embarrassed, remembering how sceptical he had been when the Dragonslayer had said they would do their best.

"You really did do your best, didn't you?" he said, adding rather sheepishly, "But then, as I said, that's all any of us can do, isn't it?"

"Indeed," said the Dragonslayer, "and I'm sure you'll do your best for us. We're rather tired, it's been a strenuous couple of weeks and we really would like a hot drink and the chance to go to bed."

"No sooner said than done. Your wish is my command," said the innkeeper, and with a few more clichés tumbling from his lips disappeared into the kitchen.

Despite the late night, they started early the following morning to try to get as far as possible before people appeared on the roads and in the fields. By noon they were out of the valley and at the place where they had seen the giant birds make their kill. The remains of the cattle beast were still there, and Jackie shuddered again at the memory of those tearing beaks. Shortly afterwards, the Dragonslayer called a halt and they picnicked under the trees.

After the meal they held a formal meeting to decide their next move. They had been well paid at Bridgeford, and the unofficial collection had also been extremely generous.

"I've got more than enough to re-equip my wife's farm," Bill said. "And I could probably buy a piece of adjacent land as well. If it's all right with you, I'll say goodbye and go home."

The Dragonslayer paid him off generously, doubling his bonus. He and Jackie expressed genuine regret at losing him. He had worked hard and very efficiently, and he had been great company. When they reached a junction in the trail later that afternoon and Bill rode off toward High Nurking and his own village, the Dragonslayer and Jackie were genuinely sorry to see him go. They rode in silence for some time, and finally it was Jackie who spoke.

"Where are we heading, and what are we going to do?" she asked. "And what about Ron?"

"Ron will probably have left High Nurking by now," the Dragonslayer said. "He wouldn't have stayed in the hospital a moment longer than he had to. He'll have ridden out as soon as he could, even if he was in pain. In fact, he's probably looking for us now."

"What are the chances of him finding us?"

"Ron," said the Dragonslayer, "has a built-in guidance system that's quite uncanny. If there was a village fifty kilometres from here, in the opposite direction to the way we came, and Ron was with us, and I asked him, 'Where do you think that village is?' he would point, and he would be right. Even if he'd never been anywhere near it before, or even heard of it until a few hours earlier, he'd get the direction right. I wouldn't be surprised to find him waiting for us at some road junction up ahead."

Jackie laughed. "Okay then. Let's just ride on south and see what we find."

They found occasional small jobs and lived well for several months without using any of their reserve cash.

None of the jobs was very exciting. Animals big enough to be a nuisance but not unduly dangerous, for the most part, and a big snake that was probably harmless, but which terrified the people of a small village. They were still finding that their fame had gone before them, both about the dragon at High Nurking and the birds at Bridgeford. It was because of their reputation as heroes that they almost missed out on what was to be one of the most interesting jobs they had ever had.

They were drinking with the locals in a village inn one night when a stranger entered and quietly listened to the conversation while enjoying a drink.

"You'd only go for the big stuff now?" he inquired courteously when the Dragonslayer had finished a modest account of the giant birds' disposal.

"Not at all," said the Dragonslayer. "It's a guild rule to do whatever work needs doing, unless there are good reasons not to. We've done half a dozen jobs since the birds, all small, but very important to the people concerned. Did you have something in mind?"

"Not really," said the man, "but perhaps in the morning we could have a business chat. It's probably not in your line, but I might as well tell you."

"Certainly," said the Dragonslayer. The man obviously did have a job that he, or someone else, wanted done, but was reluctant to speak about it in company.

The following morning he and Jackie met the man, whose name was Ivan. "I'm on private business," he said, "and I wasn't looking for a dragonslayer. But I was asked to keep a lookout for one, and if I found one to ask him if he would help us."

It quickly became apparent that he was hesitant to ask these important people to take on a small job. He was also embarrassed about the nature of the job and it took some time to get him to say what it was all about. When he did, the Dragonslayer was both amused and intrigued.

The problem was a witch. Or at least a woman the villagers believed was a witch. They blamed her for failed crops, sick stock and, more seriously, for the deaths of two children from illness. It was obvious that Ivan thought it was all superstitious nonsense, but apparent also that if she wasn't driven away things might turn very nasty for her.

"We'll help if we can," the Dragonslayer told him, "but I want to make one thing plain immediately: we will not be a party to killing her. Drive her away, yes, but no killing."

"Glad to hear it," said Ivan. "My thoughts exactly. It was bad enough when it was just crops and stock, but when the children died the mood turned nasty. Some of the fathers are talking burning. I think it's more important to prevent that than anything else. How do you propose to go about it?"

"As what we do will be largely bluff, probably the less you know about it the better," said the Dragonslayer with a grin.

"So be it," said Ivan.

He guided them to his village, three days' travel away, where once again they found themselves the centre of attention. The stories of the dragon and the giant birds had preceded them, but were much improved upon. The Dragonslayer was amused to hear that he had disposed of the dragon single-handedly. Jackie was furious. One man gave the Dragonslayer a detailed account of his hand-to-beak battle with the birds! His attempt to set the record straight was seen as modesty and further evidence of what a brave and honourable man he was. Finally he gave up trying.

When they got down to discussing the problem of the witch, the mood changed. Those who believed the old woman was a witch who had put a curse on crops and stock, and then killed two children, were all set to take the most extreme action. When the Dragonslayer pressed for a reason why she had killed the children, all he heard was, "Stands to reason, don't it? She's a witch, ain't she?"

Almost half the population, however, did not think the woman was a witch. These people were quite hostile to the Dragonslayer and his team, until Ivan was sent to pass the word to some of the cooler heads among them that the visitors didn't think she was a witch either, that they refused to even consider killing her, and that they hoped for what might best be described as a negotiated settlement.

"You're becoming quite a diplomat," Jackie told the Dragonslayer later. "If you ever run out of work, or when you get too old for it, there could be a whole new career for you. Diplomats usually get sent to foreign kingdoms — think of the good works you could do with special needs groups. You could negotiate settlements with witches and warlocks —"

"Yes, all right," said the Dragonslayer. "If you've quite finished being funny, perhaps we could discuss what we're going to do about this woman. Because if we don't do something, the father of the little girl who died is going to raise a lynch mob."

"Yes sir," Jackie said with mock seriousness.

"What I was about to say before you sidetracked me is that you've done exceptionally well since you joined me and I'm probably going to recommend to a Dragonslayer Certification Authority that you be given full grading."

Jackie smiled and went to speak, but the Dragonslayer raised his hand.

"But remember that you have to prove that you can be in full charge of a number of operations of suitable difficulty," he said. "Now, *I* don't think this woman's a witch, and *you* don't think she's a witch, but witchcraft is still taken seriously at an official level. It's still one of the compulsory requirements for certification. You could profit from this situation if you put on a good enough show. All you need to do is save the woman's life, leave everyone in the village suitably grateful, and chalk up something that'll be very useful to you. Where do you want to start?"

"By talking to her," said Jackie.

"Good. There's no time like the present, so let's get started."

XI

The woman lived in a cave on a steep hillside near the village, which was less than a half-hour ride away. The Dragonslayer noticed immediately that the patch of flat ground in front of the cave had been levelled long ago and had probably been occupied in ancient times.

The woman had heard their approach and was standing outside her cave. As they came nearer, she began to scream at the top of her voice and then to shout and threaten that she would curse them if they did not go away. She was old and stooped and long-haired, and she really did look like most people's idea of a witch.

"She's probably putting on an act to scare people,"

the Dragonslayer said to Jackie. "I wonder if she realises how dangerous the game has become."

Gathered around the old woman were the black rabbits that the villagers said were her 'familiars', or dark servants. Although black rabbits were common in some parts of the kingdom, they were unknown here, and they were seen by many of the villagers as absolute proof that she was a witch.

The Dragonslayer hoped she would listen to reason. If they couldn't persuade her to leave they would have to try to scare her, and if that failed, some of the villagers would go about it in their own way as soon as the Dragonslayer left. The thought of what they would do made him feel quite ill.

"We want to talk to you," Jackie called when the woman paused for breath.

"Go away!" she screeched. "Come closer and I'll curse you. Your hair will turn grey and your face will grow old and lined. Your back will bend like a bow and your teeth will fall out."

The Dragonslayer was not ignored.

"And your man will grow old before your eyes. He will grow weak and not be able to ride a horse or feed himself. Go before the Great Curse falls upon you. Go while you have youth and beauty and strength. Go while you have your wits, for if you come closer you will sicken and die!"

Not very consistent or logical, thought the Dragonslayer. But he could imagine the effect her words would have on the villagers, especially if what she said seemed to come true. He wondered what Jackie would do.

What Jackie did was continue to ride forward. The Dragonslayer reined in his horse and watched. This was her show.

"We only want to talk," Jackie called.

But the old woman only redoubled her yelling. She broadened the scope of her threats to include their parents (whether living or dead), their children (born or unborn), their stock (owned now, if any, and in the future) and all their friends and casual acquaintances. She promised them everything from death to a lifetime of suffering.

Still into overkill, thought the Dragonslayer. There was something not all that threatening about death first and a lifetime of suffering afterwards, but it confirmed his belief that she was no witch. She was just a harmless old lady who wanted to be left alone and had found the worst possible way to go about it.

All this time she had kept one hand behind her back, but as Jackie approached she revealed the object she had been holding. It was an antique sword that she then grasped in both hands and swung with apparent ease. From what he could see, the Dragonslayer decided it was a first-class weapon, probably perfectly balanced, and certainly not too heavy for her. And it looked very much as if she knew how to use it.

Jackie stopped her horse and dismounted. The Dragonslayer rode forward a few paces, ready to protect her. An unmounted person was less threatening than a mounted one, but Jackie had left herself much more open to attack and she had no weapon of her own.

The old woman fell silent and rested the tip of the sword on the ground. The Dragonslayer relaxed slightly. The woman had apparently expected Jackie to try to ride her down. The yelled curses started again, but now she was obviously making them up as she went along and they sounded more ridiculous than ever. In-growing toenails, indeed! After being threatened with death and a lifetime of suffering?

Jackie was trying to get a word in, over, under or in between the yelling, and was failing.

The Dragonslayer urged his horse forward two paces, just enough to get the woman's attention. When she looked at him and stopped screaming, he tried to talk to her.

"We only want to talk for a few minutes," he said. "You can talk to the young lady alone if you like, and I'll move back."

Jackie took over. "What we want to say is really important — to you. The villagers are very upset. They think you've damaged crops and killed two children. They want you driven away or even killed . . ."

It was the wrong thing to say. The woman reacted as if "killed" was the only word she understood and ran back into the cave. Jackie remounted and debated with the Dragonslayer what to do next.

They fell silent as the woman reappeared at the cave mouth. This time she wore a dark robe over her tattered clothes and carried a big book and a strange object in her hands. She came forward a few paces and laid the object on the ground. It had a peculiar and rather threatening shape, and was pointed toward them. She stepped back, opened the book, quickly found the place she wanted and began to read.

The Dragonslayer felt the hair on the back of his neck stir and was suddenly cold. This was one of the old *Books of Darkness*, dating from the days when everyone believed in witchcraft and magic was a power in the land.

"This is more serious than we thought," he said. "Up to now she's been bluffing, thinking we'd be easily scared away, but it looks very much as if she really does think she's a witch and believes in the power of curses and magic. Can you understand what she's reading?"

"It's the Old Tongue," said Jackie. "I can read it, but at the speed she's going I can catch only a few words. But I know it's not meant to do us any good."

"That's putting it rather mildly. Does it worry you?"

"No," said Jackie, "but it's not very nice knowing that someone really does want to do you that kind of harm. I'm trying to decide what to do now. At the moment I think retreat's a pretty good idea. We're just not getting through to her."

As they turned to ride away, the woman's voice changed. She was no longer reading in the Old Tongue. Her voice was unexpectedly strong and the curse came out in measured cadences they found chilling, even though they did not believe the words could have any effect.

"I curse you at board and I curse you in bed,
You are cursed from your feet to the top of your head,
I curse you at working, I curse you at eating,
I curse you at reading, I curse you at sleeping,
I curse you at coughing, I curse you at sneezing,
I curse you in poverty, I curse you in wealth,
I curse you in sickness, I curse you in health,
I curse you in walking, I curse you in riding,
I curse you in living, I curse you in dying . . ."

Her voice had risen to a hysterical scream and they couldn't catch the words of the next two or three stanzas. Then her voiced faded as the distance increased.

"You know," said Jackie, "the words weren't so frightening, really . . ."

"No, but the way she delivered them was."

Jackie shuddered. She reminded herself that the magic wasn't real, the words couldn't hurt her, and the old woman was a lot less dangerous than the giant birds or the dragon. The only immediate danger was still to the woman herself, and that still had to be dealt with.

"What was that thing she brought out and laid on the ground?" she said. "It was made of iron, wasn't it?"

"Yes, I think so," said the Dragonslayer. "She believes it contains a power, a malignant spirit, probably the spirit of a dead witch or warlock, possibly one of her ancestors. Its purpose is to focus and project her power at the target, which is why she pointed it at us. She's genuine. She knows what she's doing; she believes in her power. I think she's been stupid enough to take credit for the deaths of the children, and she probably believes her powers will protect her. They have up to now, obviously, but if that man gets a lynch mob sufficiently drunk, she may not be able to scare them off."

"I think her belief in magic can be turned against her, and I think I know how," said Jackie. "Mind if I sort out a few details in my mind before I tell you what I plan to do?"

"Not at all."

The following morning Jackie gave the Dragonslayer an outline of what she proposed. She estimated that it would take about a week to put into operation. Her plan was a bit more elaborate than he might have undertaken himself, but it was her show and she could do it her way. He agreed without hesitation.

XII

Jackie's immediate task was to persuade the believers that her plan would get rid of the witch. She also had to convince the non-believers to play along. If the believers knew that she regarded the plan as a bluff they would quibble about paying.

She spent the next two days in the home of the village scholar, a man with a good collection of old books and music who was also a non-believer who understood what she was doing.

On the evening of the second day she assembled the villagers in the inn and explained what she wanted them to do. Straight-faced, she told them that her great-grandmother had been a famous northern witch whose

135

secrets had been handed down through the family. She was careful to add that no one in the family had followed in the great lady's footsteps. Most of the villagers believed her. The Dragonslayer almost believed her himself.

It took three more days to arrange all the costumes and props, teach the villagers their parts and rehearse them, and then they were ready to go.

The next morning Jackie stood on a high rock clothed in a white gown and began an elaborate series of rites and chants. She held up objects to the sun and to the four points of the compass. She was far enough away that the witch would not be able to hear exactly what she was saying, nor see exactly what it was she held up.

Meanwhile, a gang of men cut a large six-pointed star enclosed in a circle, the traditional symbol of truth and power, into the slope opposite the witch's cave. Only the superstitious took the symbol seriously these days, but Jackie was sure the witch would believe in it, and would regard it as a power opposed to her own.

The witch came out, looked at what they were doing, then returned to the cave and reappeared a few moments later clad in the dark robe from the previous day. She carried what Jackie assumed was the same iron device, which she pointed across the valley. She then began to chant. Some of the men immediately became uneasy and carried on reluctantly only when their mates laughed at them.

When the symbol was complete, Jackie faced the cave with her arms upraised and launched into a long incantation in a foreign language. She knew the witch couldn't hear her clearly, and wouldn't understand even if she did.

Then they all went back to the village. It was an essential part of the plan that the witch should think they had done their worst and that she had been able to counter it.

That night Jackie led her trained band back to the hillside in total silence. The night was moonless and cloudy, so she was certain that the witch had no hint of their coming. A fire burned inside the cave. With some difficulty in the almost complete darkness, the villagers arranged themselves along the outline of the star and circle symbol. A few moments before midnight they set their wood and pitch torches ablaze and held them aloft. Precisely at midnight, they began the unaccompanied chant that Jackie had written after consulting the old books in the scholar's home.

Across the valley she thought she could see a dark figure passing backwards and forwards in front of the fire, but she couldn't see what the witch was doing. The chanting lasted for ten minutes, then, with the symbol still outlined in the fire of the torches, she began her own chant. This time she spoke loudly and clearly in her own language. The idea now was for the witch to hear and understand every word.

"Beyond the cycle of the days, beyond all sunlight,
    GO;
Beyond all taste of food or wine, beyond all comfort,
    GO;
Beyond the ice, beyond the fire, beyond all feeling,
    GO;
Beyond all hope of life or death, beyond all knowing,
    GO;
Beyond the moon, beyond the stars, beyond all being,
    GO;
Go without power, go without hope, go to eternal dark;
Go without memory, go without truth, go with no
    living thing;

Go forth accursed, go forth alone, *go with these words of doom*."

Many of the villagers fled, fearing that the witch would bring down the most terrible vengeance on them; some left simply because it was late and not too warm. A few waited with Jackie, watching the cave across the valley, although all they could see was the fire burning inside it. A dark figure passed in front of it a few times, then the fire faded, and was not built up again. Eventually they all went home, not knowing if they had succeeded or not.

In the morning the witch was gone. Jackie and the Dragonslayer rode out early and approached the cave with some caution, but it was deserted. A trail of footprints, made by a person heavily laden, led through the dew toward the top of the ridge. Nothing of value or interest was left in the cave.

They rode back to the village and sat down to breakfast feeling pleased with themselves, not so much for driving the witch out as for saving her life, even if she hadn't been too interested in helping them do it.

The ringleader of the believers — who had wanted to burn the witch — walked into the inn and told Jackie in a loud voice that he objected to the village paying. "You didn't do anything we couldn't have done ourselves," he said huffily.

Jackie snapped back, "No, but you didn't, did you?"

Everybody else seemed to think they had made a good bargain.

"You know, he does have a point," said the Dragonslayer after the man had left. "Or rather, he raises an interesting point. Most of the jobs we do, our clients could usually do for themselves. The dragon was an exception; that was right out of the villagers' league. But the birds . . . there was no reason why that town manager at Bridgeford couldn't have thought up the plan for himself. He was certainly capable of carrying it out."

Aware that Jackie was looking at him indignantly, he added, "But I don't agree with our angry friend. These people understood your plan perfectly once it was set out for them, but they could never have thought it up for themselves. We need to remember that many of these things look much more formidable than they really are. And if we want to stay in business, we wouldn't have it any other way, would we?"

The Dragonslayer, who was facing the inn door, heard someone enter. Feeling eyes upon him, he looked up to see Ron watching him.

"Ron!" he exclaimed, leaping to his feet.

Jackie gave Ron a welcoming smile.

"So you found us all right," said the Dragonslayer.

Ron nodded. And that was all he ever said about what had happened between the Dragonslayer and Jackie leaving High Nurking and his own arrival at the inn.

The months passed, and they found a steady stream of work. The Dragonslayer let Jackie take charge of most of it, and Ron supported her well. The Dragonslayer was pleased to note that he trusted her completely. He had treated every other apprentice as though they were about to impale themselves on their own weapons, even the ones who had in fact been doing very well. But none of the others had ever killed a dragon first time out, he thought.

One day they came to a bridge over a river that was a boundary between two kingdoms.

"Once we cross the river, do we go north or south?" the Dragonslayer asked Jackie, looking her straight in the eye so that she would know it wasn't just a casual question.

"No problem either way," said Jackie. "But if you intend to go further than the next kingdom, I'll have to ask you to do it without me."

The Dragonslayer smiled. If she was reluctant to go to the kingdom beyond this one, that must be her home. She probably knew the king of this kingdom too, but was counting on him not recognising her, or being unable or unwilling to do anything about it if he did.

"Right," he said. "We'll go south, to the capital of this kingdom, and I'll try to get you a hearing before a certification board. One can never be certain, but I don't think they'll have any grounds on which to turn you down. Not on the standard of your work or knowledge, anyway."

How they would react to a female applicant remained to be seen. He knew nothing about this kingdom and its social attitudes. Whether they had laws forbidding certain occupations to women remained to be seen.

XIII

They found rooms at an inn and the Dragonslayer disappeared for a couple of hours, saying he had work to do. He took Ron with him. When they came back the Dragonslayer told Jackie they had seen the secretary of the local certification authority.

"The man's agreed to arrange a hearing before the Dragonslayer Board as soon as possible," he said. "He'll let us know when this will be." He didn't tell Jackie that the man had raised his eyebrows in open disbelief when told that the applicant was female.

But the secretary had heard about the dragon and the giant birds, and he had looked impressed when he read through the sworn affidavits the Dragonslayer had collected from witnesses along the way. He had told the Dragonslayer that it would probably be several days before a hearing could be arranged and they would be given plenty of warning, so, in the meantime, they were free to enjoy themselves and explore the city.

There was something else. When they were walking in one of the city parks the Dragonslayer put his hand on Jackie's arm. "I wouldn't mention this if you had been an ordinary apprentice, for fear of making you nervous," he said, "but it might be important to you. Apparently it's the custom here for the king himself to confer full status on new members of all the senior guilds, and Dragonslayer ranks very high on the list. Will that be a problem?"

Jackie thought for a few moments. "No, I don't think so."

He explained that the investitures were held at public functions where possible, or else in private. The king preferred the former, but the latter could be arranged if they delayed Jackie's appearance before the board until it was too late for the next public function.

"It's okay," said Jackie. "I'd prefer the public function."

*

It was a pleasant city, much of it hundreds of years old, and the Dragonslayer, Jackie and Ron spent many hours exploring it. It was clean and neat, with a quietly efficient police force and little crime. The citizens were relaxed and friendly.

"Nice place," the Dragonslayer remarked as they walked through the busy streets.

"Most of the southern kingdoms are," Jackie told him. "It's only further north that you get the strong commercial pressures, everyone trying to make money, and the unfriendly attitudes that go with it. Have you never been south before?"

"Not into this part of the country, no. It's really quite strange to me, but I like it. Nobody's chasing us to do a job for them, though."

"Not here in a big city, and a capital at that," Jackie replied, "but I'll bet there's plenty of work out in the country. There is at home, anyway."

She looked sharply at the Dragonslayer, who had noted the only reference she had ever made to her home since their conversation shortly after he signed her on. He gave no sign that he had noticed, but it confirmed his belief that they were close to her home kingdom.

He hoped there was no major trouble coming. Taking on a princess who was pretending to be a commoner was all right in theory, and the law was on his side, but kings were *kings*, after all. People with power. People whom commoners tended to obey. Commoners like police and soldiers. Kings were people who got upset about heirs and successors disappearing into thin air. Not to mention favourite daughters. And she would be a favourite daughter, wouldn't she? A daughter who had gone missing and then turned up with a Dragonslayer who had exposed her to deadly risks like dragons and giant birds and witches. The Dragonslayer was worried.

Jackie was a little tense, too, and he couldn't decide if it was the forthcoming interview with the board or something else. Or both. Only Ron seemed unaffected. He went on being his normal talkative self, nodding or shaking his head whenever anyone spoke to him.

The Dragonslayer dropped in on the secretary of the certification authority to check that there were no problems and was assured that there were not — except that the king was determined to make the investiture at the public function, which had been postponed for a week. The secretary didn't know why.

"If she gets her grading she'll be the first female dragon-slayer we've ever heard of, and apparently the king wants to make a real occasion of it," he said.

The Dragonslayer became even more uneasy.

As the days passed, he thought he detected something strange in the attitude of the officials he met. He couldn't decide just what it was. Then, about three in the morning on a sleepless night, the thought that he might be being watched until agents of Jackie's royal father arrived to take charge of her and arrest him crept into his mind, and it wouldn't go away.

He experimented by casually suggesting to the secretary that he might have to leave before the ceremony, assuming that Jackie was given her grading.

"Oh, that would be a pity, sir," the secretary said. "Much better if you could stay."

The Dragonslayer read all sorts of sinister undertones into the secretary's words.

By the day of Jackie's appearance before the board, he was as nervous as she was and they were rubbing each other up the wrong way very badly. Finally Jackie said she couldn't bear to be around him any longer.

"I'm going for a walk," she said. "I'll find my own

way to the interview and then I'll come back here afterwards and tell you how it went."

When she returned several hours later he could see that she was much more relaxed. "I think it went all right," she said. "At least I gave definite answers to most of their questions. I remembered what you said about it always being best to have an answer of some kind. I never said I didn't know what to do in any situation."

The Dragonslayer was pleased, and he felt proud of his apprentice.

"But they came up with some impossible things, though," Jackie continued. "They wanted to know what I would have done at High Nurking if a second dragon had appeared straight after we killed the first one. Or if two birds had dropped out of the sky at Bridgeford, making three in all. I felt like telling them that I'd have called up another two hundred crossbowmen, and if they'd asked me where I would've got them from I would've told them, 'The same place you're getting all your dragons and giant birds.' But I didn't."

"Just as well," the Dragonslayer said, "but yes, interviews do tend to be like that. Remember that there are only two kinds of people on certification boards:

young ones who've never faced *any* dangerous animal, let alone a dragon; and old ones who have — a long time ago. You have to humour them as well as give them technically sound answers. I imagine you managed both very well."

"Well, I hope so. But I still don't see that three hours of silly questioning accomplished anything that wasn't covered in the affidavits you filed. I'm not sure what I expected, but something more constructive than that. You know what's wrong with officialdom? Officials!" She went off to change into more comfortable clothes.

The Dragonslayer reflected that if officials with a large sense of their own importance were all they had to worry about, he would be very happy. He was more certain than ever that something was going on, with him and Jackie at its centre, but he still had no idea what it was. Every time he relaxed and began to believe it was all his imagination, he would remember something else that seemed suspicious.

For instance, he had been asked very little about Jackie herself, which was unusual. But he was asked a lot of questions about what she had done, and what he knew about her. He had answered those very carefully, but he had the uncomfortable feeling that those answers were the ones that would get him into trouble.

So it was with some apprehension that he answered a summons from the secretary.

All the secretary wanted was to tell him that the royal ceremony that Jackie would be part of was to take place in the evening three days ahead. It seemed innocent enough until the man asked, pointedly, "You will be there, won't you?"

All the Dragonslayer's suspicions flooded back, becoming much worse when the secretary was obviously very relieved when he said he would be.

"I just need to know the numbers," the man said. "For the catering."

Again the Dragonslayer was worried. He knew it was very unusual for he and Ron to be invited to a state banquet. He was sure that it was an elaborate way of making sure they wouldn't leave until then. They would probably give Jackie her grading, then arrest him. He thought of trying to get away, but gave that idea up because he was certain he was being watched. It was better to stay around. At least Jackie would plead his case. If they let her.

XIV

hey arrived at the palace at the appointed time, dressed in newly-bought clothes appropriate to the occasion. An honour guard met them at the gates, which made even Jackie suspicious, and they were escorted inside where the chamberlain and a group of officials greeted them courteously and addressed Jackie as "ma'am", which seemed to amuse her but confirmed all the Dragonslayer's fears.

The chamberlain asked Jackie to go with a lady-in-waiting for a briefing on the ceremony, and then suggested that the Dragonslayer and Ron accompany him. The Dragonslayer knew the worst was about to happen. But as soon as he was alone with the two men the chamberlain dropped all formality and spoke quickly for several minutes. What he said left the Dragonslayer stunned and Ron gasping.

"Did you know about her, about this?" Ron asked the Dragonslayer after the man had gone. It was one of the longest sentences the Dragonslayer had ever heard him utter.

"Most of it. Not all. Her yes, this no," he said, still trying to come to grips with it.

Meanwhile, the lady-in-waiting was explaining to Jackie that the king was determined to make a great occasion of the investiture of the first woman ever to become a dragonslayer in the United Kingdoms.

"I'm not sure that I am," said Jackie.

"The king is," said the lady, and that was clearly that. She explained that the king was conducting the investitures for the other guilds at a private ceremony right now, but that he would give Jackie her cape and formal authority at the end of the public function and immediately before the banquet.

The lady-in-waiting took Jackie's hands and lowered her voice. "Now listen carefully," she said, "because this is important. When you enter, the king and queen will have left the dais, but other members of the royal family and court officials will still be there. I'll go no further than the doors. Walk straight ahead until you come to a circle of flowers laid on the carpet. Stop inside it. Curtsey to the royal party on the dais and wait for the king and queen to return. Do not turn away from the royal party while you're waiting. There'll be some activity behind you, some matters we haven't been able to attend to in advance, but pay no attention to that.

"When the king and queen enter, everyone will stand and remain standing until the monarchs are seated. The chamberlain will call you forward. Walk to the dais and up the steps and stop beside the chamberlain, facing the royal couple. The chamberlain will read out the citation, then the king will stand. You take three paces forward and curtsey. The king will then place the Cape of a Dragonslayer on your shoulders. Listen carefully to what he says, because he'll give you some important instructions. Take three paces backward, curtsey, turn, and do what you've been told."

"Which is what?"

"What the king says," said the lady, and made it plain that she was going to say no more.

*

Jackie stood in the circle of flowers trying to make sense of the muffled noises she could hear behind her. It sounded as if a lot of people were trying to move quietly but she didn't dare turn to look. The people seated on either side of the hall were watching what was happening. So were the members of the royal family. She knew some of them well enough to know that not talking was very unusual. Had they recognised her? It was, after all, a long time since they had seen her. Would it matter? She hoped not. But it might be awkward.

The mysterious noises behind her stopped. Had they been setting up the banquet tables? It hardly seemed likely. They would be placed down the centre of the hall, surely, and would never be set up before the ceremony. Or would they? And the princesses would never stop talking among themselves to watch tables being set. There was so much that was unusual about this.

She was so wrapped up in her thoughts that at first she didn't notice the king and queen enter. They seemed to take an age to settle themselves on the thrones, assisted by pages who arranged their robes. Then the people sat. After a few moments of quiet, the chamberlain's voice rang out.

"We are gathered here for an event unique in the history of the United Kingdoms: to confer the cape and status of Dragonslayer on the only woman in all history ever to achieve this high honour."

That's a bit strong, thought Jackie. I still don't know that I *am* unique, and anyway, it shouldn't be that big a deal.

The chamberlain was still talking. ". . . faced a dragon and slain it. Fought with giant birds and won. Vanquished a powerful witch. Assisted a master of his craft in innumerable challenges demanding courage and skill. I now call forward the aspirant for the honoured status of Dragonslayer to receive her cape from the hands of our monarch."

Jackie walked forward to the dais, mounted the three shallow steps and stood beside the chamberlain, facing the royal couple. The queen watched her with a faint smile on her face, but the king simply stared out into the Great Hall. The chamberlain turned to face the assembled people and read out the formal citation, a traditional document full of archaic words and phrases. Then he rose.

Jackie took three paces forward and curtseyed. The

king took the cape a footman handed him and placed it around her shoulders.

"Thus I confer upon you the honoured rank of Dragonslayer and empower you to practise your craft in all lands, with authority to call others to you and train them in the ways of your craft, according to the rules and practices of your guild," the king said in a firm voice. "It is an honour for you, but no less an honour for us. We have caused inquiries to be made far and wide and we are satisfied that no woman has ever previously received this honour. You have our congratulations, our respect and our gratitude that you have chosen our kingdom in which to take your place among the honoured ranks of dragonslayers."

He smiled for the first time. "Now you may leave us and go to greet our brother and sister monarchs."

Jackie's mind whirled. *Brother and sister monarchs? What did he mean? What was she supposed to do?*

In a daze she took three steps backward, curtseyed and turned to face the Great Hall. For a moment she felt dizzy and could make little sense of the scene before her. Could she be looking into a mirror? At the far end of the hall was a dais similar to the one on which she stood. On it sat a royal party similar to the one behind her: a king and queen on thrones, courtiers around them.

Still in a daze, she stepped down from the dais and began the long walk down the hall, still trying to make sense of what was happening. She didn't look closely at the royal couple in front of her until she was about to curtsey. Then her steps faltered.

"Father? Mother? Your Royal Highnesses," she said, dropping into a deep curtsey. When she stood, her parents rose and embraced her.

"Come and sit with us," said her father, and she saw that a third throne had mysteriously appeared between the other two. As she took her place between her parents, a trumpet fanfare announced the end of the ceremony and staff began setting up the banquet tables in the middle of the hall.

She turned to her father. "How —"

"Later," he said. "There'll be plenty of time to talk later. For now just let us enjoy being with you again."

For the first time she noticed the Dragonslayer and Ron in positions of honour on either side of the dais, both with grins so wide that she almost didn't recognise them.

*

Much later, after the banquet was over and she was alone with her parents in the guest quarters of the palace, Jackie questioned her father. "How was all this arranged? How did you know? And what happens now?"

"What happens now, or rather next, is entirely up to you. But let me start at the beginning," he replied. "When you disappeared I immediately started a search for you. I must say you were very clever. I had no idea you were going to run off at just that time, and you covered your tracks very well. It took my agents three months to find you —"

"You *found* me?"

"Of course. You didn't think I'd just let you disappear, did you?"

"No," said Jackie, "but I didn't know that you knew where I was. Nothing ever happened."

"No. I gave orders that you were to be followed, but my men weren't to act or make themselves known to you unless you appeared to be in mortal danger."

"Did the Dragonslayer know?"

"Not until tonight, just before the ceremony. All you've done, you've done on your own and your claim to Dragonslayer status is earned and genuine. But let me finish. We always knew where you were and what you were doing. We were worried, of course, especially your mother. We really would have preferred you to take on something a little less dangerous than an apprenticeship to a dragonslayer, but what my men found out about your dragonslayer reassured me that you were as safe as anyone in that trade is ever going to be.

"We didn't hear about the dragon until it was all over, which was probably for the best, but we knew you were going to tackle the giant birds long before you reached their valley. We really did worry about *that*. But all's well that ends well, as they say. I always informed the king of each kingdom you passed through that you were there, and asked them to see that you were left alone. I didn't want anyone recognising you and getting the king to pack you off home. I was informed as soon as your application was filed here. I consulted with my brother king and we made . . . certain arrangements." He laughed. "He, along with most of the other kings whose lands you passed through, was horrified and thinks I'm quite mad. Perhaps I am, but I knew what it was that drove you, and I knew very well why you had to do it."

"You did?"

"Oh yes. Definitely."

He stood up, walked to the window and gazed into the night for a few moments before turning back to her. "Remember all those stories I told you about the great expedition to the lands across the sea, and the adventures we had and the dangers we faced and the strange men and beasts we fought? You've always assumed I went as a prince and an officer, because I never told you otherwise. But I didn't. I ran away and went as a common soldier."

For once, the Princess Jacqueline was speechless.